Counting Crows

written and illustrated by
JENNI BLACKMORE

Maxine
It was crate (oops!)
I mean great, working
with you

Jenni ☺

Roseway Publishing Co. Ltd.

Copyright© Jenni Blackmore 1997

Credits
Stories, poems and illlustrations: Jenni Blackmore
Cover & book design and author photo: Karen Smith, MGDC
Proofreading: Gwen Smith-Dockrill
Printing and binding: McCurdy Printing, Halifax, Nova Scotia

Printed and bound in Canada

Published by Roseway Publishing Co. Ltd.
Lockeport, Nova Scotia B0T 1L0
phone/fax (902) 656-2223
email ktudor@atcon.com

Roseway Publishing gratefully acknowledges the support of the Canada Council and the Nova Scotia Department of Education, Cultural Affairs Division.

Canadian Cataloging in Publication Data
Blackmore, Jenni
Counting Crows
ISBN 1-896496-04-0
I. Title
PS8553.L3244C68 1997
PR9199.3.B52C68 1997

ii

For my sons,
Nikolas, Jason and Martin
With love always

Stories

Poems

v

One crow sorrow
Two crows joy
Three crows a girl
Four crows a boy
Five crows silver
Six crows gold
Seven crows a secret
never to be told

Anonymous

Fortunes Told

At first sight the gavotte Aunty Evie performs is of distinctly simian character. The words she mouths at us through the glass partition are unintelligible.

"We can't hear you!" Our shouts are lost among the breathless *there-they-ares* and the *no-that's-not-thems* of the trans-Atlantic welcoming crush and general airport hubbub.

Aunty Evie continues to cavort, oblivious to the great luggage hunt which surrounds her. Only when Uncle Will finally comes into view, hampered by duty free bags, multiple hand luggage and a wheelchair, are we able to interpret what she is saying as — He broke his bloody leg.

"He broke his leg!" says Mother.

"He broke his bloody leg!" says Father.

It is becoming quite a chant and perhaps we might also have taken up the dance performed by Aunty, were it not for the pressures of the crowd...

Step two, jump; hobble, hobble.
Back two, hands and head face heaven.
Point, point at foot. Stamp one, repeat...

By the time they have cleared customs we know the sequence off by heart. I am glad my sons are not here. I know they would be doing the dance and giggling hysterically and my father would be frowning and my stomach would be sickening as it always does when my father is displeased. I will always be his child. And, I will always love him dearly and my mother also; not merely as a duty

but as an integral part of my being. I am not ungrateful to my parents, especially as my misfortunes have treated them unfairly, leaving me fragile and needy at the time when I should be preparing to accommodate such traits in them. As further imposition on the carefully landscaped topography of their lives, my sons, their grandsons teeter along the perimeters of delinquency just as other kids cavort along the curbstones in the park. Words such as 'inappropriate' and 'moderation' are not yet part of their vocabulary and I am glad they are away, not present to revel in this situation.

Before we reach Mother's house, which is only a mere twenty minute drive from the airport, it is very obvious that Aunty Evie is no longer as we have remembered her. That's not to say that Aunty hasn't always been a little different, but previously she had managed to hide her idiosyncrasies beneath the chafing garment of middle-class respectability. Always taut and straining to tear, it's seeming now that this apparel has finally disintegrated and Aunty is left, exposed and somewhat shocking in her eccentricity.

It isn't until half way through the typically English, welcome-to-Canada supper of lettuce and sliced tomato, hard boiled eggs and canned salmon that we are able to wedge into her incessant chatter and discover exactly how Uncle broke his leg. He was pruning his favourite plum tree when he fell. It was as simple as that and yet, whether or not because of his accident, Uncle Will has changed. He is no longer the man I remember from years gone by; a man with an irrefutable air of authority which instantly transformed all manifestations of my Father's displeasure into something akin to warm pabs; a man suffused with the colour of his own experience, yet ever ready to repudiate the experience of others; a man as I recall who inclined us all to listen much and say little. Now, Uncle Will seems content to silently contemplate his toes, peeking forth from the crumbling plaster of his imperfectly applied cast and to smile benevolently at his wife's endless tirade. This change is disorienting, as is Aunty's endless flow of prattle as it dervishes along, sucking in each small void of silence, ever faster, louder and less relevant.

My gaze shifts from her, to him, to her. My affections waffle momentarily… but no, my sympathies can't be with Uncle Will because it seems to me that fate is not being cruel but merely just. Without wanting to lay blame it is hard not to think that he was instrumental in pushing Aunty over the fine line between idiosyncrasy and downright eccentricity which was drawn for her long ago, in the early days of their marriage.

Uncle Will, true to nature, had wanted perfection in his wife. He demanded perfection but she could not oblige. She burnt his food, scorched his shirts, did not care to clean and could not sew and he was not prepared for this. Neither was he prepared to see perfection in any place that he was not prepared for perfection to be. He saw only that Aunty Evie continued to muddle through as a wife and a mother and she was condemned to suffer his scorn and criticisms, even as they ground themselves like powdered glass into the fibres of her being.

Aunty's genius transcended recipe books and laundry hampers. Home-making was definitely not her forte, but fortune telling was. When Aunty delved into the metaphysical realms it was with elegance, strength and accuracy. Even as a child I welcomed her visits as brilliant cracks of light filtering into the stolid egg of my staid British upbringing. I relished every moment, treasured every word and I still remember the mystery, the enchantment, the colour in her eyes: a fragile bluer than blue, shifting like water under ice. Many times I stared through the ice as she took my hand and gently moved her fingers across its palm, leaping effortlessly back and forth through time, telling me what had been and what was to come. The final time she did this was also one of farewell; I was about to leave England, to explore the unknown, life in Canada.

That time seems so long ago. In spite of the canned salmon, the hard boiled eggs and the flattened vowel accents of the north it seems like several lifetimes past, so much has happened. I shudder at the glib elasticity of time; stretching… stretching… stretching out as if forever and then snapping back with painful emphasis. It's been too long since Aunty Evie last told my fortune. I need her to tell it again. I need her to tell me where I am going. I'm impatient to know my destiny. I don't want it sneaking up and pecking from behind or swooping down with vengeance on a day that seems like it has only to be lived through.

"Aunty, have some more tea, and I'll have some more tea and..." and then I notice the innocuous paper tags momentarily fluttering from the tea pot lid before the cozy snuggles over them like some obese woman settling down to ingest. It's not the suffocating, overstuffed cozy or the pot or the cup that alarms me, sending zigzag rays of panic down my arms, across my chest; it's the little tags of paper, each hanging from their individual string, umbilical to their own particular tea bag. No tea leaves free to float and swirl, to draw my future on the bottom of my cup? The haze of destiny rethickens, is once more impenetrable and worse, just as I am feeling so bereft Aunty manages with surprising dexterity, almost sleight of hand in fact, to spill the newly replenished cup of tea all over Mother's couch.

It is a historic moment. No one has ever done such a thing before. "Oh dear, look what I've done." The words in essence have the right meaning, it is the way they are delivered which supports my suspicion that one of the things Aunty Evie had planned to do while in Canada was to make a mess in my mother's living room.

Mother rushes into the kitchen, returning immediately with several wet cloths but Aunty is already doing penance, daubing at the wet upholstery with the voluminous silk scarf which is draped around her neck. The scarf itself is not overly gaudy but it does not go well with the dress Aunty's wearing which in turn is incompatible with the heavy floral pattern of the couch, an unlikely melange of daylilies and hibiscus against a background of petunias fraught with vines. The serenely correct British tea ceremony is suddenly transformed into a riot of hideous shape, colour and tension.

"It's alright, I've got it." snaps Aunty, by now on her knees, still daubing haphazardly with the tea-saturated scarf and obviously annoyed by what seems, to her, the unnecessary fuss Mother is making.

Mother is equally annoyed by the glaring stains which somehow manage to make themselves quite apparent upon the fecundity of the couch.

"This will work better." Mother's tone is reined in tightly but she thrusts the cloth forward like a gauntlet and the duel begins. The scrubbing is strenuous. Uncle Will wiggles his toes and watches them intently. Father excuses himself and goes to the bathroom, with the newspaper. I know it is not the time to suggest a tea cup reading.

I stand to one side, making a genuine effort to concern myself with the spilt tea, the stained couch but I'm overwhelmed with my own needs. I want Aunty Evie to tell my fortune. I want her to tell it and I want it to be good. The last time Aunty Evie told my fortune it all came true. She called things just the way they happened, but I didn't listen well enough. This time I'll listen. This time I'll listen well. Last time I didn't really know she truly was a seer and to tell the truth her words had sounded somewhat cliche although, come to think of it, she did manage to bestow upon them a certain, ominous dignity — *You will meet a dark stranger. Beware, I see blackness everywhere, all around him.*

Did she see the black fish, whales that swam up the river to die in the pasture on the day this man was born? An omen. Did she see his hair that glinted spectrum colours like a raven's wing and did she look deeper and see into his soul? I think I saw that place, but I closed my eyes and married him anyway. Did she foresee that too, I wonder. There is so much I want to ask her but Aunty is still on the floor, presenting gaudy, ample haunches, and so is my mother and they are both arguing away in the voluble tongue of body language.

For the moment I have to content myself with more memories of the last reading, how I looked at the first strand of silver in her curls that clustered, strawberry blond and how I saw the first worry lines gathering as she swirled the tea leaves in my cup with ceremony and how she continued to speak, almost apologetically — *I do see another man, also dark and very handsome. There will be a chance meeting which sparks a deep emotion. The emotion is strong but the timing is unfortunate.*

Aunty! Such understated eloquence; such accurate prediction.

The meeting was just as you predicted, ostensibly random; two strangers in a public place mesmerized by each other; breathless, wreathed in gentle ecstasy. In those first moments I saw every strand of his hair, every eyelash, every crease. I breathed in this stranger's breath and breathed it back to him. The attraction was intense, with an impact that left me reeling. Would you believe that even though I could not even guess at how or why, it was as if the story of his life passed across my eyes? Yes, I think that you would know that and also, in those moments I felt that I knew him as I knew myself and that he saw me... as I felt: transparent, vulnerable, a quaking mollusk with no shell.

Of course the timing was unfortunate. I was already married with one child born and another begun so I dropped my gaze and turned away, wanting to run, wanting the attraction to fizzle as fast as it had flashed, wanting the obsession to be over. But it would not be over. Whenever I left my house, wherever I went, it seemed that this unknown man was there, waiting. For weeks, for months, as my body swelled he hovered, casting shadows like hawks' wings over mice, seeming to threaten the existence I had so carefully constructed as a mother and a wife, but also making me feel beautiful and filling me with a desire that brought me close to tears. I could not trust myself to speak to him. Somedays I could not even trust myself to look at him and yet, I could not bear a day without the sight of him. Love? Even if I had clear understanding of that word 'love', I don't think I could use it to describe the way I felt. If I had to chose between that word or the word 'possession', along with all its inherent shadows of dark innuendo, I would chose the latter. It was a strange madness that took control of me.

Aunty Evie did you create in me a self-fulfilling prophesy? This is what I need to know. Or was it already written that this man whom I began to imagine as my soul mate, my possessor, would follow, linger, wait as the child of my husband grew within me and was born with all the blackness of his father's hair? Well, did you?

The tea is all sopped up, not a drop left. A truce is instated, unspoken but nonetheless valid, between Mother and Aunty Evie. Her wig askew, Aunty refuses to remove the tattered remnants of her scarf and we are all aware that tea will not be served again in the living room for the duration of the visit. However, the crib board is produced. Cards! Good, I'm thinking, because Aunty is equally adept at reading cards. I don't play crib but I'm quite content to watch, happily anticipating what should logically follow.

Apparently Aunty doesn't play crib either but she is not prepared to admit it. What is going on? Cards keep shooting up all over the place but she insists on attempting some elaborate shuffling technique which scatters, rather than shuffles the cards, all over the floor. I busy myself picking them up for her, feeling more and more like an unwitting observer to some bizarre plot. I know that Aunty can handle playing-cards with elegant dexterity. I've seen her do it in England, in the past. She often read my cards, and especially that last time, that most telling time, I remember very well.

I remember the frown which crossed her face like a cloud as she looked at my cards. She was silent. I watched the smoke spiral from her cigarette, gossamer strands entangling around her. A weariness gathered in her eyes as she raised them and looked into mine, then turned away to gaze again through the veils.

It was a while before she spoke. *There was a strange happening in your life that you did not comprehend and never will. You were trapped, you couldn't flee, safety was close but you remember only helplessness. That time is long gone but thoughts of it will come again. You will remember being helpless, victim, prey. You have a choice and the memory of this strange time will influence your choice. I see it in the cards that you do not make the right decision.*

That time! Of course, I immediately knew the time she meant; inexplicable, always and forever it will remain so. I was still in England, living alone in a row of houses which had been condemned. Many buildings were already boarded up and the area was pervaded with an eerie, desolate stillness. Most of the tenants had already moved away but the place was affordable and suitably squalid, de rigueur for the starving student image. I planned to remain for as long as I could, until the wrecking ball reduced the neighbourhood to smouldering heaps of rubble.

It was many years ago but I can still summon that night with exacting clarity. I still dream about it sometimes, wake up sweating, muscles aching from the tension of so much fear. The dream is always the same, nothing changes. The house is empty. I am in the attic where I live in two rooms with sloping ceilings. It is very cold. I'm trying to keep warm, trying to coax a fire in the small hearth but the coal is no good. I bought it at a little store, carried it home in paper bags, up three flights of stairs and now, already cold and weary I find it will not burn.

The night seems endless. I hear a church bell that chimes only once. How can the dawn be still so far away? There is clamour in the alleyway, a drunk falling over dustbins which are no longer owned. I hear him cursing as he wanders off into the night.

Now there is no sound. This silence is unnerving and unnatural. The very absence of noise creates cacophony. The house begins to talk freely with itself, one board to another. The fog slides in, swirling in the corners with the dankness and the dust. My ears strain for sounds they dread to hear. It is not the cold but an unspeakable fear which makes me shiver uncontrollably.

Aunty, I wish you'd straighten your wig and come listen to me, but you're busy bolstering the truce, enriching the sluicing of souls with sincerity flecked apologies. Uncle still contemplates his toes in the kitchen and Father remains ensconced. So I flash back, telescoping through the years: back 10, back 15, back 20, back to the slum, to the silence, to the fear.

It's all there, just as it was and I reach the point when suddenly, the hum of silence stops and there it is, the sound of a foot treading on the fire-escape outside. I hear a foot fall on the second step, the third; slowly, the feet do not hurry. It is a long way up that fire escape. I have time to run through the empty house, down dark hallways with doors hanging open, empty rooms, a mouldy mattress, a broken chair, nothing more… I have time to run down the stairs and down the stairs again, until I see the old front door, leaded window, fractured glass, cardboard panes… I have time to fumble with the rusty lock then out, away, never to return. I can see myself running, but I remain crouched, immobile, listening to the footsteps still ascending the rickety staircase which leads directly to my back door. Rhythmic, unhurried… step, step… step, step.

FORTUNES TOLD

I stare at the door. It is locked from the inside. There is a window in the door and as I watch a silhouette looms broad and tall behind the curtain on the glass. The footsteps have reached their destination. I wait now for the shattering of glass to break the trance, to free me, enable me to run. I wait with no heartbeat, no breath… for a crash, a shattering; tinkling shards, a fracturing blow… but there is nothing. Instead, a summer-scented breeze ripples the curtain and a hand reaches in as if through an open window and turns the knob with ease.

There was nothing more. In my next conscious moments it was morning and I was without mutilation or pain. It was only the sight of the opened door and the unbroken glass which made me wretch and weep with horror at this impalpable violation.

I never told anyone about that night. How can you describe something that you don't understand? How can you believe in something which you know to be impossible? I kept it secret but Aunty knew about that night. I never told her but somehow Aunty Evie must have known about that night to speak of it in her predictions; to refer to those inexplicable moments in my life which I will never forget, yet never understand — the fulmination of an incomplete experience.

"Well, will you or won't you?"

Aunty Evie's voice catapults me back into the present.

"Whaa… ? Oh, I'm sorry I… mm. I was day-dreaming."

"It's midnight. You can't day-dream at midnight."

"Aunty… ? No, of course not. Aunty… I wanted to ask you something. It's hardly…

"Yes. Yes. That's good. I want to ask you something too. I want to ask you if you'll teach me to crochet. Your Mom just showed me the afghan you made and it's beautiful and I want to make one just like that but every time I try to crochet I get all tangled up or it ends up the wrong shape but I know you could show me and your Mom says there's lots of wool left over and she said she'd probably find it easier tomorrow but I told her that it is tomorrow now and I don't sleep well and if I could crochet for a while after everyone else has gone to bed everything will be fine... so she's gone looking for the wool.

We talk a lot in these dark night-time morning hours but it's all about making loops and putting hooks in them and pulling threads tight. Aunty can't seem to make the thread mesh right. It won't connect, it keeps tangling, one hideous mess after another. The wool, with the hook in her fingers curls and spirals, forms impotent springs. They loll and flop down off her knee until she cuts them free and begins again, again, until finally she suggests that I take the wool and crochet a little something, just a little square, a little pot-holder maybe, that's what she'd had in mind; a gift for my mother. No one will know the difference she thinks. It seems like a good idea to me and perhaps I can draw the conversation away from the wool so that I can ask her how... but perhaps that's not the important thing right now, perhaps the important thing is that I tell her she was right.

"Aunty, I remembered your predictions. All those years later, I did meet a stranger and I was obsessed by him and by that weird night I never understood. I wanted to ask you how you knew about that and I wanted to ask you how you knew I'd make the wrong decision. How did you know Aunty?"

I hesitate, watching the hook and the wool moving together in my hands, creating something separate from themselves. She doesn't answer so I look up hoping to see some inkling in her eyes but they are closed. I won't be cheated. She has to be listening. Perhaps she just needs more information. I continue my story.

" I didn't want to make the wrong decision. I didn't want to risk my security, you know: husband, home, kids, all that stuff and I didn't want to upset Mum and Dad, you understand. At the time it seemed to me that it must have been an image of himself, a fore-runner of the stranger which had stood outside that distant door in the slum and opened it with such ease and for only one purpose, to say to me — You are not safe behind locked doors. So generous and gentle in the glow of his own omnipotence, clearly stating — You will succumb to me.

I didn't want to succumb. I was determined to remain a faithful wife, a loving mother. You can understand that, I'm sure. I was determined not to allow a spectre from the past to re-emerge and taint my present clarity so one day as the stranger stood waiting under a newly budding elm, leaves vivid green in the Spring sunlight, I walked towards him, stopped a few feet away and stared intently so as to remember every nuance of his face. His expression changed; lightened, softened. He began to smile slowly and stretch his hands out towards me as if he thought I would speak but instead, in that moment I forced myself to pretend hatred. I spat at his feet, raked him with a withering glare and a snarl of rage before I lifted my head in an attitude of complete disdain, turned on my heel and marched away. I never saw him again.

So you see Aunty, once again your predictions were impeccable and it wasn't long before that became apparent. First of all that blackness you foresaw, it swallowed the man I was married to, or perhaps it merely surfaced from the depths of his being, left there by the black fish who swam up the river and beached themselves in the pasture on the day that he was born. I believe it was a curse that clung like bitumen, suffocating all else, contaminating everything it touched. It touched me and it touched my sons. We're all stunted now, not just me, but they're good kids really and I think you'll like them when you meet them. Anyway, I blame the black fish and I guess I have to blame myself as well. I should have paid more careful attention to your predictions, especially about that night in the empty house, when the hand reached in through the window and I smelled a breeze. It smelt like summer, but at the time… well, I understand it better now, and do you know, during all those years of misery and abuse I often stood under that elm tree and ran my fingers over the rugged bark, wondering if I could have re-directed destiny just by opening my arms and smiling at the stranger. Of course it's too late now, but I'd still like to know. Do you think I could have done that?"

Aunty Evie doesn't answer. She's snoring gently, slumped down in the easy chair. I cover her with the afghan she admired, feeling a certain affection along with sharp pangs of annoyance and disappointment. I had so wanted to know if I could have cheated fate. When I saw her performing that primitive mime, weaving through the throng of travelling propriety, I should have known that her spirit also had been choked with tar and that her mind was such that she wouldn't remember how she knew that I would make the wrong decision on that day when the stranger waited beneath the elm tree for the final time.

Frogsong

I heard the first frogs tonight, singing in the little patch of swamp that no one wants to build on. They caught me off guard, amazed me somewhat. I had come to believe that this winter would last forever.

JENNI BLACKMORE — COUNTING CROWS

Those frogs, though very much involved in their own pursuits have affected me greatly. They have discounted the wetness still trying to be snow which seeps into my shoes. They have told me that this is the first day of Spring, not that slushy, grey day the calendar proclaimed. I am giddy with relief. What Summer could have followed such a day?

It is the right of frogs to announce the time. It is for them to sense the indefinable changing. They are so much closer to the real beginnings, with instincts not yet cauterized. They feel that deep earth tremor, that subtle shift in rhythms prior to birthing. Even these dogs of mine, they sense it too. They pull harder as I walk them down the lane. The mongrel chases Fat Cat with renewed vigour and judging by her howls returning, is rebuffed with similar enthusiasm. It had seemed for a while that this game was losing its appeal, perhaps due to the simplicity of the rules, the predictability of the score: fat black cat feigns acquiescence; feisty mutt, enticed by the promise of some small victory, slips all restraints in hot pursuit, soon to return, painfully defeated yet again. The fat cat remains unconquerable but as we walk home, (score not tallied, as not for quite a while now) I keep that froggy chorus chiming in my mind, sandwiched as tightly as the dog's tail is wedged between her haunches.

The house is illuminated as it usually is, with no available light left unlit. It has the aura of a pleasure boat viewed at night and somewhat vulgar in its ostentation. This is not contrived effect, but merely the result of carelessness, a lack of discipline. We do not need to draw attention to our position, especially in this neighbourhood of discreet lighting gleaming weakly through demurely shaded windows. We are so obviously misplaced in this safe grey settlement of suburbanites and their uniformity magnifies our flamboyant incongruity with typical preciseness.

From here on the street I have often gazed in through their windows, longing for the sanctity of their ordered

17

lives but tonight I look at my house, the one we've shivered in throughout this winter; the same house I often dread to enter, fearing to confront the ricocheting tensions, the ribald energies which wreathe my adolescent sons. I look at my house with its undressed windows, its naked bulbs burning, its disarray of wounded vulnerabilities exposed and tonight it seems right that I should call it home.

For the first time I note that it may not be the swamp that no one cares to live by but in fact this place of turmoil, my house. And happily I realize that as the neighbourhood pariahs we inadvertently protect the place of frogs, the earth mother clock of joyful heralding. Frogsong fundamentalists! A not unsuitable appellation; Defender of Frogs, those engaging metronomes who have been known to count the measure in this scheme of mine.

In the other life time, the one no longer mentioned, the bloody, bruising, painful time of connubial chaos, of marital mayhem, in the early days of that life, there were some joyful Springs (which are dangerous to remember lest they cloud true memory); Springs of frog songs and gentleness when we would lay entwined, entranced by the mystery of the voices floating from another world, sounds of an ancient community engrossed in ritual, revelling in their pageant of love, their annual celebration in the little patch of swamp.

Soon that landscape changed, was irreparably scarred by a senseless, indomitable force that filled in that primordial space with clay and rubble. I cried for the crushed and mangled loves, both mine and theirs, as the music of their mating was replaced by the grating screech of order imposed upon the lyrical chaos of life. But all of that is past and with the rubble stomped down tight, compressed, solidified, there is new building ground which hardly ever moistens with its previous fecundity.

In memoriam, of swamps gone by, in recognition of my newly established, fundamentalist vocation there can be a secret sign, an inscrutable symbol; not a fish but a frog to be chalked on the door and the walls and the pathways to this house. I will be your champion, swamp dwellers. I, matriarch of the pariahs, Defender of the Frogs! No one will move too close to us. No one will come claiming the dark void of your dwelling place.

In retrospect, in some future time I will read the devious scheme between these lines. I will recognize the style. I will see it is the Pooka of Euphoria releasing red balloons in the cactus colony of my existence; equipping cats to lure this mongrel mind of mine but for now, frogs, I will defend you. I will remain as a deterrent, a protector of your space and you in return will be my helium on nights like this. You with your singing will lift me above the unpaid bills, the miscreant sons and the bed, cold and lonely because I am damaged, just as my children are damaged, well beyond a certain point of loving.

Princess Rose

Silly Labrador lying on your back
  trying every trick to get acclaim
    and all because I'm speaking to frail bones bundled
  albeit most brilliantly in feathers

    And when I parrot, Beauty-beauty, beauty-beauty,
    you squirm and wriggle, paws skyward
    and when I say, So sweety-tweety-tweety,
    you jump erect and say, Yes me! Yes me!

    I'm talking to the bird you know
      the one with tongue truncated that does not seem to salivate.
    Okay, I didn't mean to sound that way and truly,
    when you kiss my hand, my Princess Rose
    I know I have been kissed

  Looking at your eyes, brown, soft, moist
  above white quarter moons that plead, Love me,
  I understand that love is endless, boundless, unprejudiced
as much for feathers as for fur

  Love is immeasurable, appreciation without bounds or bonds
  hypnotic awe, transcending the mundane
  and love is, my Princess Rose,
big enough to nurture both you and the bird

The Wages of Love

"He's dying O.K. So just get upstairs and go to bed."

The dog lay in the hallway, breathing hoarsely, eyes open but seeing nothing. Above one eye, where the car had hit, some fur was missing but there was no blood.

It's an invisible wound — with clinical detachment this thought was all that came into the woman's mind and she stood, trying to determine exactly what it was that flowed through her with all the efficacy of ether. Yes, an invisible wound she decided, as she looked at the dog's inert body, but lethal nevertheless, releasing cataracts of death which gushed inside him. Even as she watched the sheen seemed to be leaving the black fur.

"Do something Mum." The boy spoke quietly from the top of the stairs. He had always seemed weaker, less boisterous than his older brothers and as she glanced upwards the woman was startled to see how frail and vulnerable he looked.

"Go to bed. I told you, there's nothing I can do. The dog is dead."

"But he's breathing", the boy insisted.

"The lungs haven't stopped working yet. You know about chickens that run with their heads cut off? This is the same thing. He's like a chicken that's running without a head. It's the same thing."

Same thing? She questioned the voice as it spoke. Where was it coming from? Where was this rock hard place of logic and simple rationale? And where was the weeping, the unbearable ache in that soft, warm place of soul? Where was all that? Had she not loved that pup? and had it not reciprocated with full canine capacity; with an unquestioning adoration, powerful enough to guide the dog home even when it was as good as dead?

She could hear the boy crying in his room but she felt too dry, too numb. She couldn't go to him. Instead she stood watching the dying dog, wishing that she could also cry.

God, I'm getting hard, she thought.

Finally the breathing stopped. She picked up the phone intending to call someone, to tell them about the dead dog, to ask them to come and move it. Surely this was a man's job, to come and dispose of the carcass. She could be a mother and act as father but not as undertaker; this was too much to expect of her. Surely, there was someone she could call? But no, there it was again, the unyielding, insurmountable wall of simple fact — there was no one, the onus was all hers. It was her dog and her responsibility.

Replacing the receiver she walked into the kitchen and automatically stuffed some bed sheets into the washing machine. At the very moment when the dog was hit she had been thinking about beds, beds with lovers in them; specifically her bed. After so long, she could barely remember the minutia of that scenario. With a surge of panic she had been trying to restore fading memories and to justify her desires by weighing loneliness against the impropriety of substituting lust for love.

Just as she had been deciding that a lover would be good for her, a necessity in fact, it had happened. Her beautiful Labrador, the one that worshipped her; her dog, that she loved dearly, was running or perhaps just walking slowly, nose to ground, in front of tires on that same ground. All in an instant it was over. Really, it was over in that instant, the rest was merely effluent.

The machine began to agitate, wrestling down a blue and white bubble of dirty bed sheet and slowly the rawness began to

THE WAGES OF LOVE

expand its perimeters within her, tearing apart the centre of her being. A suffocating haze of thought moved in to fill the void of her consciousness, questioning: Had Pup done penance for her anticipated promiscuity.

Back in the hallway the dog's eyes had dulled to be almost indistinguishable from his black fur. She felt a twinge of revulsion at the thought of having to touch his body and wondered if she could do it. Tentatively she reached out a finger and attempted to close one of the eyes. The eye remained open but at least she knew she could do what had to be done.

She could touch the legs. She did not shudder as she felt the claws and the pads of the feet brush against the palm of her hand but she wanted to avoid the head; didn't want to touch it. Didn't want to look at it.

The dog was heavier than she'd expected it to be and it flopped like water in a rubber sack as she tried to slide it gently into a large plastic bag. The bag was not large enough, the head protruded. She tried to slide a second garbage bag gently under the soft muzzle without looking at the moist nose gone dry, the tongue no longer licking but it seemed the dog was trying to claw its way out of the bag and she had to look and as she looked the magnificent head suddenly rolled around to face her squarely, eyes wide and accusing, jaws falling open in a grotesque, silent bark.

She could feel the familiar cracks beginning to travel up the wall. Time was running out. Roughly, quickly, she shoved the head into the bag, no longer caring about respect, just needing to be done. The body was heavy and fearing the bag would rip apart, that the dog would be on the floor again, she was forced to carry it in both arms, to cradle it against her like a sick child, until she reached the porch. There she rummaged for an empty box, while thinking how she didn't want garbage bags and cardboard boxes for Pup.

He was the only velvet in her life.

Later, when she went upstairs, the boy was in the bathtub watching a television propped precariously on the wash-basin.

"When things like this happen you just have to close your mind to it. Do you understand?" Her jaw tightened and her eyes narrowed to force back unexpected tears. "It's not going to make any difference to Pup if we remember him or not."

"I know Mum. I'm okay now", the naked boy mumbled. His attention returned automatically to the television but the sight of his mother, his sudden sense of the indefinable depth surrounding her, caught his gaze and jerked it away from the screen. "But what about you? Are you okay?"

She turned quickly so he wouldn't see her face and nodded. She wanted to say, sure I'm okay, but tears began streaming down her face and she held her breath to trap the sobs as she closed the bathroom door behind her.

She was in bed, lying naked between the clean sheets when the phone rang. She knew it was the man she had been planning to sleep with. She didn't want to answer but he kept redialling until finally her anger matched her grief and she snatched up the receiver by her bed and screamed into it with her pain and anger crashing out on giant breakers of profanity. He didn't call again and she was left with an immense vacuum that sucked in upon itself as tightly as a clenched fist with every breath she took.

Pulling the covers over her head she curled tightly into a foetal position. When she slept she dreamt about love and how it became obsolete because it always hurt. And in the dream she paraded with a placard which read — The Wages of Love are Always Pain.

Beer for Breakfast

In the early, very early
morning hours
between the time
that hookers count the cost
and nuns awake
the stillness is profound

Nothing moves
except for dogs with fleas
truckers
and myself
confronted with the choice
Will it be Wheetabix or beer?

And with the bottle emptied
my trickster spirit grins
crouching to extol
with puckish glee
vindicating vice as virtue
calling 'free-will' this game's name.

a dysfunctional story

I'm going to write a story tonight. Going to string words like pearls; going to structure a plot with a middle sandwiched in between a beginning and The End and I'm going to drink some beer, for creativity's sake. Going to write this story out happy.

There is a boy called Ben. He can be one of the characters. Ben is thirteen wishing he was nineteen. His brother is sixteen. This boy's name is Aaron. He can also be a character in the story.

I have opened my second beer. It's going down faster than the first and it really does taste good. The desk light illuminates the bubbles as I refill my glass. A large fly is also attracted by the light. It's fat and it buzzes loudly. Flies are lethargic at this time of year and I pick it off the curtain with a tissue and squash it with my fingers. Is this some kind of foreshadowing? an integral part of the plot?

In my story there are two brothers. One is called Ben and one is called Aaron. The plot can be quite simple. The oldest boy, Aaron, does a lot of stuff — like hash and grass and he drinks heavily, most of the time. He always has plenty of money but he doesn't have a job. The plot thickens.

Perhaps this will be an interactive story. Does Aaron deal drugs to support his habits? Why does he do this? Was his father an alcoholic? Did Aaron love his father despite his cruel and violent nature? Is Aaron in fact an anti-hero who refuses to abandon his quest for some just reciprocal of love? In this story, is Aaron a thoroughly messed up kid? Is it the fault of his mother? Should she have left the alcoholic father before he had chance to damage his sons?

The third beer tastes good and it's only two a.m. It's kind of late to be starting but I want to get this down, don't

27

want to forget it and if I keep on writing I could have a good story here, especially if I develop the characters more.

Ben is thirteen. He does not do well in school. His main interest is in girls. His mother does not attempt to interfere with his natural instincts, however, she is glad she has sons and not daughters. If she had daughters she wouldn't want them sleeping with the Bens of this world. Or the Aarons. They don't treat girls well but the mother remains loyal to her sons despite their actions.

I've opened my fourth beer. Feeling good about this story; really getting into it; think it has potential. So, Ben knows that his brother deals drugs but whenever his mother gets suspicious he lies and covers up for Aaron. Perhaps he doesn't want to hurt his mother by telling her the truth or perhaps he doesn't want to rat on his brother. Perhaps he hopes Aaron will straighten out, but in this story Aaron doesn't do that. (There's some subtle, psychological stuff happens here. I haven't quite figured it out yet but I think it will be about siblings and love and hate and rivalry). Anyway, Aaron keeps on dealing and he keeps on doing drugs. In this story Aaron gets to be in pretty bad shape.

The third character in the story has to be the mother. She is not very smart. She should kick these boys out. She knows what's acceptable and what's not but for some reason she seems unable to see her options clearly. Perhaps she needs glasses or perhaps she just needs to open her eyes. This is a weak woman. She keeps feeling sorry for herself and making too many excuses. Does she feel guilty about not leaving the alcoholic husband sooner? Yes, that would make sense. That would help explain why she chooses to believe her sons' amoebic lies, their monosyllabic untruths which multiply ad infinitum.

Did I mention my fifth beer? That's not what this story's all about but I am lining the caps up on my desk so I know how many beers I've drank and where the story's up to.

Let's re-cap. This story is about a mother who has two sons. Neither son respects the mother. Perhaps the father taught them this; no matter what he handed out she still went back for more, so perhaps, is this the mother's fault? Is this story about abuse and weak women who perpetuate its cycle? No, it's not! What about golden glasses of beer filled with endless streams of tiny bubbles, rushing upwards from an unknown source to the heaven of their effervescent universe; is that what this story is really all about? Definitely not. It's about a mother and her sons.

Those are the three characters; a mother and her two sons. Will three characters be enough? I could introduce a man the mother meets somewhere. He is very high on something and keeps mistaking her for a character out of a Thomas Hardy novel. He discusses in depth the fact that his sweater is not pink but peach in colour. This seems to be important to him. His breath smells of vomit but even so the mother briefly considers the possibilities of a relationship with this man because she is lonely and needs to feel arms holding her sometimes.

No. The man in the peach coloured sweater wants to be in a story but it's not this story. If he were in this story he would have to jump in and separate the brothers when they begin to fight and he's not strong enough to do that. No, there's no place for him in this story. What about a third brother? A younger brother? No place for him either. Hide him under the bed. He's scared, so leave him there.

In this story there are only two brothers and a mother and when the brothers begin to fight there's no one there to separate them except the mother and she's too busy crying. Why is she crying? Is she crying because of the hash and the money strewn across the table? Is it there because there's been an expose? Has Ben finally exposed his brother Aaron? Is the mother crying because she has been forced to face reality? Perhaps she is crying because her son Ben is crying. And Aaron? well, he's smiling. He's very high and we're not sure how much he understands about what's going on, so his motivations will remain obscure.

Ben is crying from anger and perhaps from love of his mother and his brother, but mainly he's crying because he just wants things to be different. He weeps from rage and sorrow and in his rage and sorrow he screams out words his mother has never heard him use before. The tears stream down around Ben's nostrils and drip from the corners of his mouth. He appears to be very strong and magnificent as he weeps. And the mother? She doesn't know why she's crying anymore. In this story she just cries a lot.

There are now nine beer caps lined up on the desk before me but actually I've only drank eight and a half bottles. There was another fly. He wasn't as lethargic as the first fly and some beer was spilt as I swatted around with a wet towel. The towel was wet because of the shower I've just taken. I showered because my eyes are sore. Often when I'm in the shower I stretch my arms out above my head and place the palms of my hands together, fingers outstretched like I'm praying, but I'm not praying. I'm trying to touch that certain, centered space in the deluge where there's nothing coming down on me. Sometimes, if I drink enough beer, it seems like I can be in a place like that and other times I just get very tired.

I want to end this story now. The characters have gone flat and the beer's run out on me so it can be a multiple choice ending. Maybe everything works out okay in the end. Maybe the mother figures out how to get tough and whips the boys into shape or maybe she just becomes an alcoholic because she spends too much time trying to shelter from the rain. The End.

A DYSFUNCTIONAL STORY

Blind Date

a feather
shells
and grass?

from Earth and
Ocean…
don't confuse me man
i'm a woman
and all i want is love

Messages in the sand
me?
with you
laughing, dancing,
prancing

I'm telling you
don't fool with me
i'm just a woman
and all i want is love

Cosmic seduction?
don't mess
with my cosmic, man
I am a woman
and i only thought
I needed love

Yes. I am W O M A N
and I want
to know why
i needed you
to tell Me that

Silent Shore

What is this stillness?
blanket stifling
keeping hidden
all that is

Where's the wind?
to tear this sorrow
clinging, draped
like spider's thread

Wave made thunder
where are you?
come drown out
these crying sounds

But maram stands
by mirrored water
and water mirrors
sculptured shards
and all is stillness
nothing changes
in this deathlike
lethargy

Playing God

Moon rising
almost whole
one cycle's sliver gone
Waves playing
stones in swell
a noisy silence this

Bugs falling
on the page
backward spinning gyroscopes
enchanted by the light
needing finger touch to turn them
brush them gently on their way

Moon rising
Waves constant
in their rhythm
Bugs still falling
taps on paper
no finger touching me

Indian Summers

Late in the afternoon a subtle indistinctness transforms the landscape. Unlike the mists and fog which blow in off the ocean, sometimes thick enough to obliterate, sometimes to merely blur, this phenomenon is too volatile to be identified. It gilds with a soft-edged cast of unreality, as in a shrouded memory or a half-forgotten dream.

They are coming, just as they always come creeping, sneaking along, feigning obsequiously; a half-hearted attempt to disguise their malicious arrogance — diminutive figures, faceless under hooded robes.

An ominous stillness seems to paralyse the waves and hangs heavy over salt marsh and soft wood growth beyond. The stillness is intense; even rodents and insects lurking in their habitats are motionless, not because they rest, but because they wait.

Coo and warble like doves, shriek like monkeys, giggle with malevolent glee. As you prance around me nimbly, swirling robes reveal your sinewed limbs and waft odours of deep diggings.

In the stillness, the almost invisible haze is a nuance, the first hint, Earth's warning that the change is coming, the warmth of swelled-until-bursting Indian Summer days will soon be gone and not with gradual transition. They are not committed to sneak away or faze out gradually. Theirs is always a guest appearance and as guests they can come and go as abruptly as they please.

Warm flesh cringes at the touch of parchment covered bones. It is them. It is them! My soul screams as they tighten the seasoned leather around my wrists and ankles. They push me, drag me, goad me backwards, buzzing and swarming like bees who will have me in their hive and without pity they strap me once again onto their wheel.

The departure is imminent and the mother gentleness of Earth gives warning that her softness will soon be harsh and un-accommodating. Frozen barrens will be where unruly over-growth now flaunts itself with all the arrogance of imagined immortality.

And when I am strapped securely they cavort and twitter and stumble against each other, such is their excitement. ROUND AND ROUND AND ROUND SHE GOES… they chant as the wheel begins to spin and I am sucked into the vortex of my own memory; spinning, spinning, spinning… AND WHERE SHE STOPS…

I am in England, revisiting my home, introducing my parents to their grandsons. We are all together, playing football in an urban park, a grubby green clearing amidst the forest of factory chimneys and blank faced, brick facades.

The first born is seven, overawed and certainly overjoyed to be doused in such unquestioning adoration. He wants to excel, to become worthy and retain, but also just to wallow in his por-tion of grand-parental love.

He kicks the ball. This is how I can win my Poppa. And Poppa kicks the ball. This is my grandson. I think he will be famous, perhaps a soccer star if we work on it early enough. And Momma follows the baby, whose short, chubby legs propel him after the ball with Chaplinesque dexterity.

The ball leads them gradually, farther and farther away and I watch my parents and my sons enjoying moments of pure happiness, encapsulated in a vague haze of atmospheric change. The air itself seems almost visible and the surrounding stillness is so noticeable that it bespeaks of a most sombre religious occasion. And so it is, this day of suspended motion, of yearly farewell, when

Summer and Fall relinquish all claim and Winter moves in suavely with all the feigned benevolence of a dictator.

I will it to be that I can stay in this place. I will it to be. I will it to be, but slowly the wheel begins to turn again, spinning ever faster until the vortex sucks me back and the pointer hits the spindles which circumscribe the wheel; clatteratteratter clatter clatter claa... ter claa

My belly is swollen. I am in the time when I have not yet been called mother and I'm walking with the father of my unborn child. Dahlia stems sag under the overabundance of their blossoms, their eagerness of colour which tries but cannot mask the frost blackened foliage.

We pass an elderly couple strolling, hand in hand through the park. They walk slowly, oblivious to the glances they attract, engrossed in each other and very much in love. They are neither quaint nor comical, but exquisitely elegant and everyone who walks by determines to be just like them if they should have the fortune to live that long. The man I am with verbalizes his desire. He wants me to confirm that, yes, indeed our love will remain powerful, untainted, and that, yes, fifty years from now we will resemble the elderly couple.

I assure him that it will be so, even as I know I lie. Do I will what is to come at this moment? Let me change things here. Let me say yes and believe it. Let me keep this time because it is a good time as we wander hand in hand through this day of unnatural warmth and stillness, precursor to the season of bitter furies.

But again the wheel is spinning. Faster, faster and then slowing, slower, clatterclatter clack claa... Keep going, not this square! No, no not this square... and the pointer listens, it presses against the spindle which marks transition to another time but the velocity is gone. The wheel is weighted and holds still on its wellgreased axle. The pointer flops back, impotent in the space it never can bypass.

There's a yellowness here, old bruises under fading summer
tan and newer ones of purple and some blue; rainbow remnants
of the ritual. Strange things to notice as I lie naked in my fear. I
feel the floor scrape as I'm dragged across it, the burn of the stuc-
co raking flesh as I am thrown against the wall. I feel… very little.
I am a walnut hidden within the chest cavity in a place that only I
know of.

Words don't hurt the walnut. What are words but letters and sounds
and what are they but marks on paper, vibrations in the air? Physical
pain: livid finger prints indented into flesh, purple eyes swollen
shut, bleeding lips, torn hair, it all means nothing to this little nut.

I gaze beyond the raging demon as his hands tighten around my
throat. Over the shoulder of his hugeness I glimpse a corner of the
window with sunlight shining through. Dislocated thoughts,
recalling other walnuts; childhood memories, Christmas times.
Such a struggle for the nutcracker; shells so rigid, so staunch
that some, only a hammer could fracture into submission. And
it was not always pure, untouched meat they protected but
sometimes only the musty blackness of decay.

I am running. Rag doll with walnut stuffing running to the
shore, needing wind and crashing waves to restore the
life source in the kernel of my being. But it is the day of
change, the passing of Indian Summer. The stillness
impresses me like a tightly wound shroud, encased in
pine and trapped in dirt and I sit motionless, without
thought or feeling, slowly dying from the inside out.

37

Make this wheel spin. I am suffocating, gasping, pleading. Make
this wheel spin and get me out of here… and finally I sense the ini-
tial tremors of culmulative motion. This time when the wheel spins the
pointer stops at NOW. Winning square. I can quit while I'm ahead
and watch them scurrying off, cursing and foul under their breath,
tripping and panting as they carry the wheel away to their place of
safe keeping.

I drive slowly into town, absorbing the stillness and the warmth. The sun sinks as if for the last time and the sky bleeds with the agony of goodbye.

I will meet the man I am to dine with. He will say, you're quiet tonight. I will tell him the shrapnel is bothering me. He will frown enquiringly and I will explain, an old war wound. Exploding walnut shell. Little men will rush about in his head, reinforcing his defenses, sounding the alarm and he will consider dating the secretary with the diminutive breasts while he smiles at me attentively and pours the wine.

Old Bones

I'm walking to the past on the shale beside the shore
with a sorrow that weighs heavy;
tricked me, caught me unawares
and clings now to my back.

I sit at the lagoon inviting it to rest
perhaps remain but it declines and we continue,
into water, me wading wishing it was
deep enough for drowning.

The old dog has forgotten, swims ahead, leaves chevron wake
towards the shore where tail flags expectation;
hugs, kisses in this place which tolerated wet dogs
curled up close beside the nightime fire.

The crows divide the silence, each one takes its share
as dog lunges through the scattered boards
to find only the saw, abandoned and already wooed
by moss, which dulls the bite of rusted teeth
with stifling caress.

No laugh, no shout,
no echoes bending rusty nails in scavenged wood.
The boys have gone dog.
The fort no longer stands.

The Day of the Kamikaze Caterpillars

This is a simple story about a mother and her sons. For no apparent reason the facts have been encroached upon; various insects crawl and squirm between the words. Even inside the house several fat flies buzz with arrogant nonchalance. Having survived the first frost they seem to think that they will live forever.

In the window, a spider with a grossly swollen abdomen hangs centred in its web but the woman gazes past it, absorbed by the sparkle of sunlight on ocean and the thoughts which are seeping into her consciousness like so much spilt milk.

Yellow warmth on water. Gentle touch. Sensuous. Mmmm. The kind of touch I miss sometimes. Like a lover not quite able to tear himself away, kissing once and one more time again; lingering, just like summer in September, unable to succumb to the inevitable. I have been there, kissing, being kissed, but strangely, passion does ebb, just like this ocean, no matter how much one might will that it should stay.

On this September morning there is that same breathless warmth, the kiss of sun still loving Earth long after the rites of fertility have accomplished their design.

Caught by a breeze the web outside the window vibrates and her attention is drawn towards the spider; an already pregnant mother bouncing violently with copulating rhythms, soon to give birth to a myriad off-spring. She knows all about spiders and their progeny. She shudders as she remembers.

Spiders! They were everywhere in that cabin, originating from one yel-low fluff ball tucked in the corner of a grimy window pane. When they

THE DAY OF THE KAMIKAZE CATERPILLARS

hatched, spewing forth, a multitude of minute insects slowly fanning out across the glass, the boys had wanted to destroy them. I was the one who said to leave them be, so there was only myself to blame when they hung from every sooty beam, spinning diligently in every crack and corner, attaching guy lines everywhere. They scurried across my pillow, in my bed at night, and were no longer babes but bulbous six legged, creeping crawlers. Then the boys refused to destroy them and merely quoted, most gleefully, from my previous equanimity — They have as much right to be here as we do.

Is it only a year ago that we struggled to survive in that place? God, I don't know how we did it, but indeed that cabin was both the worst and the best of the places we lived in. To call it merely rustic would be to lie; it was squalid and oh, so very cold. No plumbing, no warmth or comfort, but at least it marked the end of our journey as it squatted there like some ugly unmentionable beside this place, the glorious, rising edifice of our new home. What a time of transition! And me, alive again, always encouraging the boys, keeping them warm with dreams about how beautiful our new home would be, while all the while I was hardly sure myself it could be so. I'm surprised they believed me. In truth they were a little old for such trusting naïvete. Ben was almost eighteen then and Matthew, well younger certainly but still old enough to be more pragmatic.

They believed because they wanted to believe, needed to believe. They were still shell shocked. We all were. You don't need to go through a war to get that way. Living with their father was enough. Emotional destitution. That's what set us apart. It caused us to wander for years like some urban dispossessed until we finally figured it out. To have a proper home again, to have a proper life again, a unity, a coherence, we had to build it for ourselves from the foundation up. And finally we did. It took a while but here it is. Here we are.

She stretches an arm and slowly trails her fingers down a cupboard door. Though only one year passed that winter of hardship spent in the cabin seems light years removed from the pristine kitchen with its oak and ceramic styling.

Beautiful house, with so much peace in it. Life is now as I never thought it could be and within myself also, swelling like the most voluptuous peony about to bloom. He is gone forever; no trace, no place for him here. Even when he tries to come, sneaking in my dreams, poised naked, reeking of vengeance and power I see him only as a gaily decorated pinata with a grotesquely exaggerated phallus. Ha! And that is what I strike at first.

He is gone from me. No more threatening now than scattered candies on the ground. I am healed. The wound is finally mended, albeit darned with wire. But I am strong, resistant to pain. Sometimes it was cheese wire, clinical and clean, cutting deep when tugged on; sometimes barbed to tear flesh ragged and often rusty, insidious, causing flesh to fester but even that pus has oozed and drained away. Seven years, magical number. Finally I am healed and in this stillness I can feel the flower within me bloom.

She breathes deeply and exhales with a sigh which whispers joy and gentle ecstasy.

Distant barking heralds the two dogs running on the beach, obsessively chasing gulls along the surf. If their object is to actually catch a bird they seem undaunted by their lack of success. Not unlike her sons with their gargantuan capacity for pursuing unrealistic goals, she thinks and wonders if they are still asleep upstairs. And even as she thinks this her mind hesitates then tentatively reaches towards a vague notion. She strains to recall the earlier sleep-filled hours: had she heard one of them return home at three or was it four that morning; stumbling and mumbling, falling against the wall? She dismisses the thought as just another nightmare, another ubiquitous shadow from the past but the mood is broken and she turns away from the window, pads barefoot down the hallway, through the quiet house where even the sound of the waves comes muted, seemingly hesitant to enter and interfere with this Sunday morning silence.

The shattering of this peace is visual. She sees that several

43

large canvases, already prepared for paint and stacked against the studio wall have been shifted haphazardly to reveal a camp stove, some unclaimed residue of summer's visitors. The lid of the stove hangs open. Tutored well by years of traumatic conditioning she immediately recognizes the space inside for what it is, a clever, clandestine storage place which was emptied sometime through the night.

Anger on disgust upon dismay, all teeter above a fearful, nauseating need to know if it was hard drugs, soft drugs or only alcohol which had been hidden in the space.

Only alcohol? Instantly she recoils. Only alcohol? Hah! She jeers bitterly at herself and as penance forces herself to remember her son as she had seen him several times, soaked in urine with his face pressed forward into blood flecked vomit; and as she had found him after her frantic search along the railroad tracks, sleeping with his head resting on the moonlit steel; and on that freezing night when she had dragged the dead weight of his body from the snowbank to her car, wondering all the while if she was already too late. She questions bitterly how she could still think of it as being *only* alcohol.

Torn between anger, fear and dismay she rushes toward the stairs which lead to the boys' part of the house. She wants to barge into his room and drag him from his bed, confront him with the evidence, evict him from her house, her life, her memory.

The first she is sure that she can do, the second, maybe she can, but the third, never. There would always be the questions. What if she'd been more patient? What if she'd given him yet one more chance? What if she'd let him stay, with his swarthy handsomeness already tainted by dissolution; with his smile no longer genuine but more a smirk, a curling of the lips; his fingers stained with the residue of nicotine and other drugs; his knuckles crushed from pounding walls and people, a stolen ring on one finger and her discarded wedding band on the other?

What if she lets him stay despite all this? Will he heal eventually as she has done? She sits down on the stairs to struggle with the choices; angry words clanging down steel shafts sunk into the tissues of her brain, echoes from the doctors, the counsellors, the specialists.

Don't forgive him! You can't keep forgiving. Got to be tough. Tough Love! Can't let him get away with it. Can't keep forgiving.

Don't forgive! Easy for them to say. Forgive who? My child for his need to escape reality? The man I married who I am still loath to call husband, father? Or is it men the collective I should not forgive for their transgressions? What is this word forgive to me? I prefer the theory that only God has that option.

Do not forgive him — kick him out — legally he's a man — old enough to stand on his own. Sure, it's easy for them to say. He isn't their son. They never saw him as a little child, innocent and loving, coming home from school with smiles that always turned to tears. They didn't see him spurned, rebuffed; again, again, again; always on the rebound, like a rubber ball against a wall, his father with the racket. And the drunkenness, the violence; they didn't see him watching that with disbelief and lack of understanding.

So, what if I hold these memories as my excuse for his being like he is and my excuse for being weak, not wanting to let him to go, not wanting to face the reality of the situation? When it comes to reality, the more I try to determine what it is, the more volatile it becomes. Surely there can't be a single, true reality to any situation because reality is based on personal perception. That entity — reality — as I am coming to understand, is not at all concrete but highly abstract and subjective, representing nothing more than an individual opinion of what is happening. I think we all can choose our own reality.

45

With this in mind the woman decides to believe that this son is taking longer to heal than his brother and herself have done. She chooses to believe that there is within him also a tightly bound peony bud already swarming with ants, satiating themselves on the sweetness of his pre-blossoming excretions. She decides that this will be her reality.

She taps gently on both bedroom doors, wakes her sons and tells them she is going to the farm for eggs; promising to make omelets when she returns. She thinks this will give him time to re-group himself, clean up, replace the camp stove and the canvases. Now that she knows one of his hiding places she can at least judge the nature and extent of his addiction. It is better that he doesn't know she has this source of information.

The coastal road, always scenic to excess, snakes by silver water that steals her gaze and at first she doesn't see them. Not that it would have mattered, they are everywhere and impossible to avoid. A colony of kamikaze caterpillars is crossing the road; thousands of furry little worms arching their way from one patch of marram grass to another, travelling towards some figment of their own reality.

Road-house Requiem

Another dog died in my arms today. It's becoming almost a reg-
ularity, this kneeling in the roadside mud, cradling a dying mutt
and I'm developing an immunity to the pain of it all: the wishing,
hoping, praying that the beast won't die while knowing all the

while that it will. Today I didn't cry. I didn't use that trite, that hackneyed but adequate phrase — oh, my God, why did this have to happen? In fact I didn't say anything at all. Which, it could be considered, was handling things quite well or most peculiarly, depending on the point of view.

It's a dirt road we live on and I was smeared in mud and blood and not saying a word. I did noticed that my blouse was unfastened, revealing a good part of my breast. My hand searched independently but for some reason it couldn't find the buttons. People gathered; six or seven neighbours and friends and their kids and my kids. They thought I was in shock but I wasn't, I was just putting in the minutes until it was all over; suspended, without feelings and with no thoughts to voice.

I didn't chose or practise to become so callous. It was a gradual process, a survival technique. As a family we don't have great luck with our pets, especially with regard to their longevity and it's good that the kids and I have figured out our own ways to handle this. I'm not sure how they do it but for me, suspended animation is the key. It's like I turn down the volume in the sad parts. Certainly the trauma has seemed to diminish with each mishap. The first few casualties had a much more profound effect and probably the most memorable for me was caused by the death of the Afghan hound. That death and my ensuing grief caused me to confuse my dreams with reality which is seldom a happy circumstance.

Actually, the Afghan didn't die an untimely death. He grew old, incontinent and arthritic and it was time to determine that he had lived long enough. Perhaps his opinion differed. However, I drove him to the clinic and led him to the room, crying profusely all the way and I held him to me as the needle pierced his vein and that was it. Life, gone so easily, sliding away within seconds, to some-where. Perhaps there could have been a sense of power, of the lesser god variety, or at least a subtle feeling of relief couched in the bland finality of dog death but for me there was only self loathing.

I hated myself and that night I went out in search of absolution. At first I felt awkward and highly visible sitting in a bar, alone, but I had watched death that day and after the first couple of drinks I was able to be more objective about what matters and what is irrelevant.

The place where I drank was called The Road House and I considered this appellation as I sat at the bar, assuming what I considered to be an air of sedate yet casual relaxation. I tried to compose an accurate definition of the term 'road-house'. A house by a road where liquor is served was not specific enough, it lacked the transient quality that permeated the atmosphere and saturated the patrons as much as did the alcohol. Finally I opted for — a stopping place along the highway — as the interpretation most devoid of any sense of permanence. That was where I was, to drink, in the jostling, smoky, crowded anonymity. Such was the reality, the place where my true identity, that of executioner, could be checked in with my coat; temporarily abandoned for a price.

Price. In a word there lies the problem. I never go for the economy, quick fix. My choice is always the expensive, long on payments, emotionally bankrupting solution. This time his name was Charles. Not a complete stranger, but an erstwhile knight returned, a prince from the past whom I had once believed would whisk me away from the depths of my abysmal marriage and into the blinding whiteness of eternal happiness. He never knew this of course. I'm sure he never suspected the exotic and erotic scenarios he inspired; endless variations on the same theme of our eventual togetherness. To him I was always and only the wife of his business associate. That's the way it was. I became a dreamer and he, though totally unaware of it, became my escape route from the dismal reality of my marriage. That dog dying day was the first time I had seen him in years. I was no longer married and yet still unfamiliar with the various interpretations of my role as a 'free woman'.

When I met Charles in The Road House I didn't question why he was there or why he was somewhat less than sober. It wasn't the sort of place I'd assumed he would frequent but I simply took it for granted that fate had finally intervened with typical whimsy by bringing us together in the most unlikely spot imaginable. Perhaps his dog had died too!

As we danced the floor throbbed with an endless disco beat and the strobe lights spun circles of multi-coloured webs and spinning with them I abandoned all realities in favour of my dreams. It seemed right that he would hold me, that his lips would brush against my ear and finally press themselves against mine, making passage for his tongue. The tawdriness of The Road House was blocked out by the beauty of shimmering light, the past seemed suddenly very distant and the future, during those suspended moments shone, indistinguishable in its own brilliance.

It was all as I'd imagined it would be, pristine and ethereal until the semi-sober greyness of the early dawn when he left my bed with words only of regret and apprehension. I was still my husband's wife, he bleated with genuine fear, despite the divorce, despite the intervening years. I would always be my husband's wife and he must never know what had happened that night, according to the leaven of all my dreaming. It could always be our little secret, couldn't it? he begged.

In the long term it was good that he whimpered away my dreams and much of my naïvety, but after the fact I wanted to explain to Charles that if that night hadn't been the tail end of a dog dying day I never would have confused my dreams with the reality and if we had met under any other circumstances it would have been quite sufficient for him to merely buy me a drink.

Tonight, as some funerary mode seems obligatory, it seems fitting that I should remember other dogs from the past and listen! Is that the distant echo of the pack? I am trying to suppress my smile in view of the solemnity of this occasion but there's an irrepressible joy which stems from the knowledge that my flesh is safe tonight, even though jackals still hunt and dogs keep dying and heartaches will always flutter in the gloom, searching for a place to call their own.

Howling Dogs

This is a song for the moon
and all the dogs that bark at it
a song for brutal men
who satisfy their lust
a song for blood and bruises
fractured limbs and broken trust
This is a song for the moon
silent witness in the night

This is a song for the moon
and all the dogs that bark at it
a song for battered women
smeared with sperm and tears
a song for empty promises
withered hope and wasted years
This is a song for the moon
shining sister seeing all

This is a song for the moon
and all the dogs that bark at it
echoing through an endless night
the terror of their reign
a song for fear and cruelty
that chokes out joy and nurtures pain
This is a song for the moon
of changing seasons, turning tides

Charts and Journeys

I was swimming off the coast of Corfu when the thought came to me. Well, that's not quite correct, it was more than a thought; a thought can be fleeting, almost transient whereas this was a realization; the sudden knowing that it was time to continue my journey.

I'm not speaking of the superficial travelling I was involved with at that moment, the meandering through Europe with a sweet and tender man, but of the more arduous journey. I refer to my search for the place where I truly belong as a woman in freedom and relationship. I had a fragile, shifting memory of this place from long ago and I needed to go back there but the chart had been destroyed.

Past encounters had eroded so much of my being that it seemed I had also lost the ability to distinguish between what was acceptable and what was good and destined just for me. Accepting anything which did not hurt with an almost bovine gratitude had become an easy habit but at that moment as I swam, I felt suddenly encouraged and empowered to want more.

I swam the length of the bay, knowing that I could also swim the length of the next bay if I so chose. I looked at the brown arms parting the water in front of me and it was at that moment I saw myself, as if for the first time. Just me, free from the trauma of the past, me with a new chart in hand, able to go wherever I pleased and to do whatever I chose. Feeling the water sliding softly over my body and letting the sun make rainbow prisms in the droplets on my eyelashes, I knew that it was my time to stand alone.

53

When I returned Paul was asleep, with his lean body laying face down on a straw mat. There was something very young, very vulnerable about his neck, his smooth skinned shoulders and the mask and snorkel lying by his

JENNI BLACKMORE — COUNTING CROWS

side. For the first time I loved him more as a mother than as a lover. I lay down quietly by his side on the other straw mat and wondered how I would explain why we had to part. I pulled at the straw which was beginning to unravel, remembering how we had bought the mats on a beach in Italy. I don't remember the name of that little Italian town. I only remember it as the place of intangible and yet gross sexual insult such as I had not experienced before.

The name of the town is not important but I do need to recall the black man on that beach because somehow he is a factor in the progression; a geometric aberration with hostile points securely accommodated in the crazed paving of my yellow brick road.

I had seen him before, wandering along the sand trying to sell woollen sweaters and pseudo designer jeans. I was discomfited by the incongruity of his merchandise and the fact that no one was buying. I empathized with him, wondered why he didn't offer more suitable items: suntan lotion or beach towels.

It was still very hot there in September. Paul had gone to prepare our usual meal of bread and cheese and fruit with yoghurt. I remember clearly that it was the place where I first encountered fresh figs, with their innocuous pale green skin, splitting open so innocently to reveal the ultimate pleasure; seductive, natural sweetness such as I had never tasted and colour swirling with the white yoghurt like alizarin red and thalo purple smeared together across a virgin canvas. That was the food which was being prepared as I lay alone on the beach, waiting in heat deadened anticipation.

When the shadow first crossed me I thought it was Paul returning with the lunch. I stirred and looked with an expectant smile towards the figure silhouetted against the blazing sun, but then I saw the feet and knew it was not Paul. I particularly remember the feet. They were large, calloused and dusty from walking in sand that powdered the very blackness of their Ethiopian skin like flour.

I remember his feet well because I looked at them as I shook my head lazily at the proffered woollen sweater. I thought that would be enough but he didn't move and I gazed at his feet as he towered above me, blocking out the sun, until their image burnt into my memory. And still he didn't go.

I turned over onto my stomach, pretending to read the book I had by my side but I could feel his eyes ripping away the pink cloth of my bikini and I felt the pressure of his erect penis as strongly as if it was being rammed against my naked buttocks.

To escape this sensation I shifted onto my back again, feigning an attempt at sleep, thinking that bravado, pretending he was not there would make him go away, but he didn't go away and I cursed the dense black tendrils which seemed to twine like magic vines, escaping the insufficient cover of my pink satin crotch. As I lay, effectively naked before his eyes, I peeked only at his feet which were gnarled with callouses and cracks, intimate recordings of his lifetime's walking without shoes.

The man didn't go away and after his shadow had lain across me for several minutes I looked up at his gaunt face. His eyes stared unflinchingly back at me. Momentarily I was confused. The fine hairs on my body raised up from salt damp skin. The look in his eyes was familiar and despite the heat I shivered. I had seen the same expression once before, in blood shot eyes suffused with rage but where? Where? Slowly the memory expanded like pixels on a screen and the eyes became many eyes and I saw bars and discarded peanut shells. The vision kept expanding, encompassing the more cunning zoos where bars are disguised by landscaping, cages camouflaged to placate the squeamish, to protect them from olfactory clues but the smell remains the same, of hopelessness, the excrement emitted from proud and magnificent beings held captive, unable to fulfil their given potential and with nothing to nurture but rage and frustration. A malevolent essence, it was there, in all the eyes.

The vision faded but still there was the man, the Ethiopian. I lay there at his mercy and in some way a willing sacrifice, feeling a responsibility to compensate for his hatred and his pain as he stood and raped me in his anger without so much as touching me. My degradation was in no way diminished by the absence of his touch. The vendor was all powerful and remained so until he turned and walked away with regal indifference when Paul finally arrived with the food.

It was on the Italian beach that we bought the straw mats. They travelled with us, constantly unrolled, re-rolled, absorbing our sweat and stray fibres of our journey, a lazy zigzag South, East, South and then West until we arrived on the Island of Corfu. The heat was still intense even though it was late in the season. I was nauseous from cheap Yugoslavian wine, consumed on the ferry, and drained by the heat and confusion of the crowded bus station. Eyes, mouths, voices: matronly breasts swelling under black cloth, wrinkled brown skin, lips drawn tight and thin: men's eyes, like subtle fingers forever undressing, tobacco stained smiles and heat in visible streaks swirling through the simmering turmoil.

The bus was packed and we were fortunate to get seats. We both needed to sit but Paul soon offered his place to somebody's grandmother. *What a nice boy*, the thought flickered in her eyes as he swayed and stooped in front of us, trying to look through the windows and keep his footing as the bus careened through the dusty countryside. *What a nice boy*.

Before this ancient woman scurried off the bus like some engorged, black-winged insect she took Paul's hand and pulled him down towards me so that we were once more sitting side by side on the back seat of the crowded bus. A Greek bus, a bus where people socialize, joking and laughing, where they sing and argue, eat and drink and indulge their erotic fantasies.

Though not tall, the man who assumed Paul's standing space seemed to tower above us. Directly in our line of vision, he effectively blocked out all view of the interminable olive groves and we had little choice but to stare at the profile of his sex. When he first began his sensuous gyrations I found it hard not to laugh. Instead I coughed and pushed my palm against my mouth.

The man's tight jeans emphasized what he obviously considered to be one of his more redeeming features. The rest of his body was short and subtly disproportionate, almost simian. Most disturbing was his smile which was reminiscent of ancient jaw bones, the fragmented remains of our predecessors.

At first glance the woman who wedged in by him was almost beautiful, with strawberry blond hair cascading down her back in lose curls. However, on closer inspection she too displayed subtle incongruities which gave her a certain ugliness in equal measure to her beauty, an apparent freakishness which was hard to define.

The bus swayed and rocked vigorously. She moved with it, holding tightly onto the overhead hand grips. I wondered if Paul would forfeit his seat for a second time to this woman but I sensed that he didn't like her. I imagined how he would categorize her: has never believed in dragons or fairies, will always be sceptical of love and is expert in at least ten sexual practices. Her aura was tarnished but she did also exude a childlike wholesomeness which further strengthened the anomalous impression she created, nevertheless Paul remained seated.

As the bus swayed and rocked the man rubbed the front of his body against the woman's back. Soon her spine began to arch as she pressed her buttocks closer towards him and moved her hips rhythmically from side to side. Her head went back and the golden curls brushed against the man's face. He put his tongue out and pulled a lock of her hair into his mouth.

Aided by the rocking of the bus their movements assumed the mesmerizing beauty of a dance, as they writhed and pressed their bodies together in pre-orgasmic oblivion. The other passengers seemed unaware of this overt eroticism and before my eyes the tawdriness of their public display evaporated, leaving only a residue of sexual purity.

Finally the bus reached its destination and everyone disembarked. The man began to walk away and as I watched, the woman turned and started out in the other direction without a word.

I kept their ecstasy with me as I swam in the warm, turquoise water, knowing that their incidental coupling was at one end in the maze of human relationship where I must strive to find my destined place among the narrow corridors of misogyny and concupiscence. As I lay next to the man I planned to leave, I wondered if he would understand when I tried to explain and I wondered if I would regret being lured away from his safe haven by murmurs from lost empires and vague memories of unconditional happiness.

59

Paper Boats

Happy
  I want to be happy

    I want to lie in sleep
    and dream of escargot
    swelling imperceptibly
    in spiralled opalescence

    Happy
    just to be happy

     to hear the sound of breathing leaves
     and watch the shadow of the sun
    move slowly by the lunar face
    to worship new hatched feathers as they dry
   and taste the sweetness of ripe figs
  mixed hues… purple, green
 seeds pith skin
delirium

  That's how happy

 watching fragile boats
 float distant on the tide
overloaded with the hurt
that renders me preoccupied

JENNI BLACKMORE — COUNTING CROWS

Morning Song

Special morning
after rain
early heat
engenders steam
magic motion
hypnotizing
silent spell
tranquillity

Rhythmic music
in the garden
dripping branches
sparkle green
Insects busy
feathers flutter
feeding children
in the nest

It is time
to gauge perfection
set the fulcrum
of existence
senses tingling
clearly seeing
this the central
core of being

With a Grasshopper
on My Shoulder

It always seems to me that people tend to think I'm much smarter than I really am. There's something about the way they pay attention to what I say that makes me suspect that I am the only one with a clear perception of my intellectual capabilities. They are very limited. My mind is not concise, important facts swirl through it like tide flowing through a net. I'm often appalled by the amount of information I forget, at the number of times I encounter knowledge which used to be mine until I lost it somewhere along the way.

My brain also has no ability to reason unemotionally or to retain numbers in any form or sequence. While some people can memorize their license plate number I can't even remember what year my car was made in. When I'm driving it's not unusual for me to forget which country I'm in, which side of the highway I'm supposed to be on. In truth I am a hazard on the road and it worries a little to be so absent minded. I believe that much of my problem stems from a dysfunctional memory which is exacerbated by an innate urge to do stupid, irrational things.

Interestingly enough my most recent stupid mistake made me feel rather good about myself eventually. It happened when I was walking on the beach with my youngest son. He'd been away all summer with his grandparents and I hadn't seen much of him so we were just hanging out together. Everything was fine until I got uptight and started snapping at him. Truth was I wanted to go off on my own and have a cigarette.

I quit smoking fifteen years ago, it's such a disgusting habit. I hate the smell and the taste and all the self-destructive concepts that cigarettes support, so of course I was not pleased with myself for getting hooked on nicotine again. In fact I hated myself for smoking which was why I wanted to sneak off on my own somewhere so my son wouldn't see me performing such a demeaning ritual.

He wouldn't leave, even when I got nasty so finally I told him the truth about wanting a cigarette. This was the first stupid mistake because he knows what it means when I smoke. It means that I'm weakening, that I can't take things anymore, that I don't care anymore and when I smoke it usually means that I'm going to drink as well. He's only twelve but he understands a lot.

Matthew's a cute guy, kind of shiny and expectant looking, with freckles and a toothy grin. His head was shaved pretty well bald while he was away by some butcher barber and this noticeable absence of hair made his ears seem even bigger than usual, which in turn gave him an awkward, vulnerable look. When I told him about wanting the cigarette and all the muscles in his face sagged with disappointment, his aura of terrible sadness was multiplied at least ten times over by the obscene haircut. It shocked me to see him look that way. I hadn't expected him to be so crushed over one cigarette.

At that moment I felt very guilty but nevertheless sat on a bank of eel grass and puffed like crazy, wishing I could smoke three at once, while he walked off along the beach looking dismal. He was gone for a long time and for all of that time I looked out at the ocean, which glistened and was very beautiful that day and I wanted to be part of it all but felt somehow separated by the nicotine thing. I tried to figure out why I had smoked the cigarette and why I had be so stupid as to hurt my son like that. There was no excuse for it so when he finally returned I asked him to forgive me and I told him that I'd try not to smoke anymore. He shrugged his shoulders but he still had that look on his face, so then I begged him to forgive me and I gave him the rest of the cigarettes in the pack to destroy and also my solemn word that I wouldn't ever smoke again.

I had to think hard about it because I wasn't sure that I could keep such a promise but I knew I'd have to if I didn't want to see him look that way again. I guess he knew I meant it because his face finally brightened up and he viciously ground the remaining cigarettes into irretrievable particles between two rocks.

I said, "Thank you Matthew. It's a good thing you're around to smarten me up when I get stupid and guess what... it makes me feel great to know that I don't smoke now".

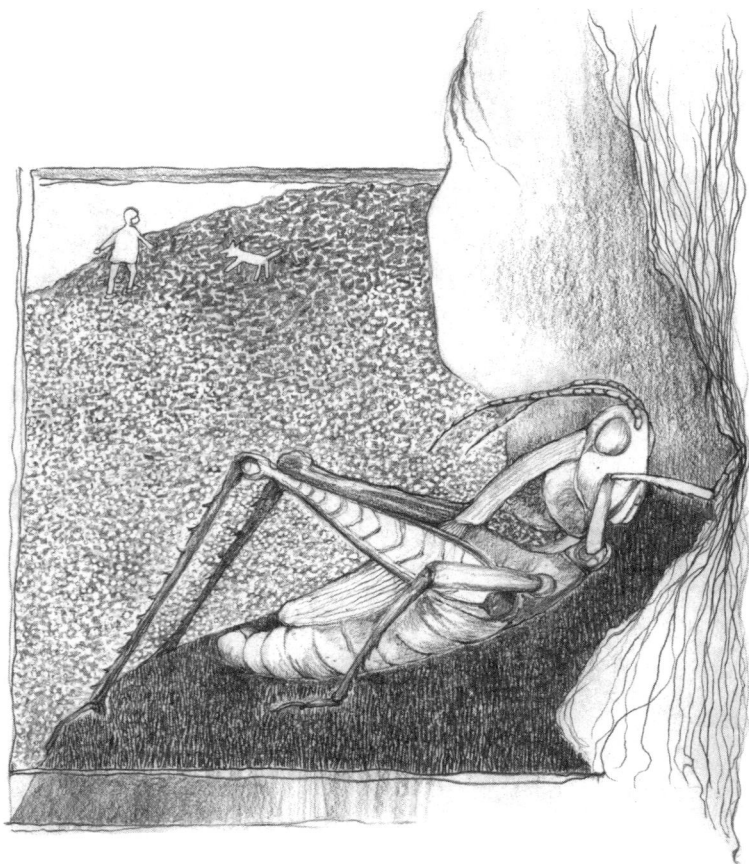

And it did feel good. I was relieved that I couldn't smoke ever again and the more I thought about it the better I felt. In fact I felt so good that I got really excited and I kept hugging my son and thanking him, as we walked along the beach.

He was happy. I was happy. Everything was fine until one of our dogs started to roll on top of a dead seagull and I threw a rock to scare the dog away. The rock wasn't meant to hit the dog. It was just meant to scare her but because I have such poor aim the rock hit the dog and she started making a terrible noise, much like a donkey giving birth. It sounded like she was going to die and I didn't know what to do so I started walking around in circles with my hands over my ears saying, "God, I didn't mean to do that".

Matthew was right behind me sounding very distressed as he kept repeating, "I know you didn't mean to do that, Mum". I guess he also thought the dog was going to die and it did seem like she really was because she kept lying there braying, so I kept on with the spiral walkabout, Matthew following close behind step for step, until the dog finally gave up on trying to get any sympathy and ran off along the beach after the other dog, just like nothing had happened. What a ham!

"I don't believe how incredibly stupid that whole scene was, " I apologised to Matthew.

"Yeah. It was kinda', but it was pretty funny when you think about it", he said and began to laugh.

We continued to walk for miles along that endless beach in the brisk warm wind with everything shining, so clean and pure. It was a most perfect day and the beach grass was full of grasshoppers jumping around like crazy as if in celebration of it. One jumped from the grass right onto my blue sweater. It was brilliant emerald with orange legs and so perfectly formed that it looked like a complex plastic toy. It seemed quite content to journey along on my shoulder and I felt specially chosen.

By the time we turned around the sun had disappeared and the wisps of cloud were turning red against the darkness of the sky. Only the waves and the sand they kept wetting remained visible, lighting a way for us to follow and my son and the dogs ran ahead along this shining path.

I started to get the strange feeling that builds up in me sometimes. It's a hard feeling to explain; almost an excitement, an exhilaration that threatens to grow very powerful if you let it. Sometimes I'm too scared to let it, but at that moment with the grasshopper on my shoulder, I just kept letting the feeling flow into me until my whole body was charged with an intense energy. The effort of walking became so negligible that I was oblivious to it, so much so that I seemed to float. My mind became similarly affected and I began thinking the way I used to think when I was very young, knowing exactly how things are without a doubt, understanding the very essence of everything. For instance, when I came to a place on the beach where boulders are washed over by waves I understood exactly how they felt. I could feel it too. It's like a caress when a wave washes over a boulder, very gentle and meaning everything. It was then that I realized that I'm not altogether stupid. I just have a different kind of knowledge.

By this time it was completely dark and even the thin silver line of the water's edge was hard to see. I could hear Matthew in the distance, calling for me to hurry and I had a sense that the grasshopper was still on my shoulder, but being very quiet. Not smoking didn't seem like any kind of a big deal at that moment because for the first time in a long while I understood quite clearly that I can do just about anything I choose to.

Returning

The first thing she noticed as she entered the house was her father's jacket on a nail by the Keymac stove, hanging rigidly as if he were still wearing it. Once the best of oilskins, it was now cracked and scarred by age and abuse.

"Christ! Why did he have to hang it so close to the stove?"

The same old irritation rose in her as she tried to rationalize her father's stubborn, wasteful ways but quickly faded. She was too weary for anger. She wanted a drink and wondered if the local boot-legger had managed to outlive his best customer.

"Why go to town and give mi' money to the godamn government when I can walk down the lane and buy from mi' best friend Bill?"

"Your best friend, hah! He charges twice what you'd pay at the liquor store. He left you to freeze outside your door. You think he cares about you?"

"You want a drink or don't you?"

That had been the gist of their last conversation. Ten or was it eleven years ago? She couldn't remember.

"Yes, I want a drink Daddy. I want a drink now." And for a moment it seemed that he would be there to take the bottle off the counter and set it down with a certain finality.

67

The way her father put the bottle on the table had always carried a certain inference. When she was very small it had seemed like it was a special beginning, intro-ducing magic that would make everyone merry. But soon she saw it more as a challenge. There was something in the way her father looked at the bottle, the way his hand lingered momentarily, barely touching it that seemed to indicate he expected something but was never sure when it would come. As a kid she had chosen for a while to believe that he was waiting to see the last bottle, that he was in fact questioning each one as he placed it on the table, *"Can I quit after I've finished you?"*

She stared at the centre of the table where the bottle would have stood and once she had the bottle clearly situated the rest of the scene was easy to recreate: several men sitting around the table and her father taking her on his knee like he never did when they were alone and her mother, gaunt, pale faced, leading her off to bed and tugging extra hard at the ribbon in hair; the laughter downstairs gradually turning to argument and the men knocking over chairs and cursing as they staggered off into the night and herself laying with her breath held tight, waiting.

She had the scene off pat. Her father's shouts, her mothers sobs, the bumping of her mother's body dragged and goaded up the stairs and finally his snores and her mother's muffled sobs. And she, as monitor of the situation could then relax and finally sleep. It was a simple formula but it had been known to go awry: too much bumping, mother's screams too loud, complete silence before they went upstairs, these were all signs she had to listen carefully for. They meant that something had gone wrong.

The woman had never mourned her mother. She blamed her for allowing the father to be the way he was. At church she saw women with husbands who sat docile, with collars starched stiff enough to hold the men's heads up even as they dozed. Some of them were big women, but some were even smaller than her mother and they could make their husbands behave. So why couldn't her mother make her father be like that?

He allowed them to go church. Their weekly entertainment, as he put it, but when a new minister came to town and zealously started making his rounds her father thought that things had gone far enough.

"Be warned. I'll not have any clergy meddlin' in my home life."

Not knowing any differently the priest came to visit anyway so her father chopped the tires of the parish car, then rambled off over the pasture with the axe on his shoulder and a torrent of curses roaring from his mouth.

Her mother gave a little laugh and asked the minister if he would have some more tea. He was very young and his face had turned red and was twitching on one side from his cheek to his nose but he gave a weak laugh, almost identical to her mother's, and said, yes indeed, he would love some more tea. And when he was leaving he told the woman she was a lucky girl to have a mother who made the best biscuits and yes indeed the best preserves in the county. And he called her, little lady, and told her to look after her mother.

"Oh God! This is ridiculous. I drive five hundred miles just so I can do a number on myself? Look at this place. She chose to stay here. She could have fought more. Did she ever really know what it was like in school after the tires got chopped? I don't think so! It's forty years Ma, but I could you tell exactly what it was like, right down to the last snigger."

69

A large fly, sole survivor of the winter's cold, buzzed erratically against the warmth of the window pane. In the silence of the empty house the drip of melting snow outside sounded loud. The woman walked across the linoleum, following the path, worn black and free of the pattern which still clung to the less travelled corners of the floor. She opened the door and discovered once again that there was indeed another world out there. It was one of those magical days that sometimes come in the middle of winter, the kind of day when jackets get dropped in snow-banks and forgotten and so much snow is melting all around that it sounds like a symphony.

Eventually she retreated from the glare of the sunlight and returned to the scarred wooden table, its history laid bare by the gouges, scars of naked wood darkened with grease and dirt and circled with rings of different coloured paint. It was the dark green she remembered most clearly, having stared at it so often and so hard while suffering the torments of their evening meals. The family of three; mother, father and child seated with their food before them waiting for the fury to unleash itself and engulf the table like a fireball. The ten-sion was so powerful it would almost choke her, drying her mouth, constricting her throat, but she dared not swal-low hard because he could ask in his carefully measured voice, the one he thought controlled the slur of alcohol, his pious and indignant voice, the voice he always used at the start of a meal, after the initial pause of silence when everyone was pretending it wasn't going to happen that day: then he could ask, in his carefully measured voice, what was wrong? Why did she seem so tense? Didn't she like to sit at the table with her father? Perhaps she didn't think he was good enough to eat with? And where did she think all the food came from? And did she think he enjoyed working all the hours God sent to feed an ungrateful brat who wouldn't sit at the table with him? And didn't she think he knew it was her mother who put her up to it?

The fury would build its momentum like pressure in a boiler wait-ing to be released by the throwing of a plate or the tipping of the table. Indeed, she had learned not to swallow hard or to look down or to look up or to smile or to be serious, to eat too slowly or too fast but it didn't make much difference because there was always his faithful standby:

"You'd better eat your fill and make the most of it because God knows you won't be eating like this when I'm dead and gone. Before I'm cold she'll have someone else. That much is for certain. Some no-good bum that'll move in and enjoy everything I've slaved for. Yes, you'd better enjoy it now while you have the chance. You think I'm gonna' work 'til I drop so some no-good bum can move in here? You think I'm godamn crazy do you? Well, do you?"

The prospect of the no-good bum taking his place unleashed the fury quicker and more violently than any of the misdemeanours the child tried so hard to avoid. When his anger had run its course and he had stamped out of the house; when her mother was clearing away the wasted food with trembling hands she would sometimes seize her daughter by the shoulders, staring into her eyes like a madwoman.

"Don't ever live your life like this, girl. Don't let anyone make you live your life like this."

There were worse times. There were times when the fury didn't make her mother tremble, times when her mother's eyes seemed to shrink back into their sockets and lose the moisture that made them shine and when her father raged she didn't seemed to hear. She didn't do the things he told her to and when he hit her she didn't seem to feel it.

For a moment the woman can see her mother dragging herself across the floor, father is kicking her but she doesn't seem to feel it and she looks up and says,

"Don't ever live your life like this girl," and there's another voice, a little voice pleading, *"Not now Mamma, please don't say that now"*.

The sound of her own voice broke the woman's reverie as her fingers still explore the gnarled table with the telltale traces of green paint.

RETURNING

"No Mamma, I won't ever live my life like that."

The ocean shone, a colourless glare and last year's beach grass, bent by a sudden wind, etched circles in the snow. A family would buy the place, she thought, and the children could pick wild strawberries in July and carry shells and rocks up off the beach. Perhaps the father would be kind and the woman no doubt would love him. Those kind of people could be happy there she thought. It was possible.

Her sleek car looked incongruous on the pebble lane. It glinted invitingly and she was relieved to settle into its plush interior. The muted click of the door locks was reassuring and the cell phone at her finger tips gave easy access to her preferred mode of communication. As she drove away she thought how stark the real estate sign would look against the weathered shingles and the lonely beach.

Atlantic Low

Walking alone
along a dead end track
towards the sea
with only the swallows
to protest my presence
among the salt-cured shanties
clustered on the rocky shore
I have seen the sky
a clear cerulean echo chamber
with my spirits rising to it
but presently
enigmatic cloud lowers the ceiling
and greys the waves
to match the chillness of the wind
and my own emptiness

73

The Great Bird of Sorrow

There's a great bird
hatched by demons
Sorrow is its name
been on my shoulder
long enough
time to go bird
can't remain

Listen!
Creak of ancient wings
archaeopteryx ascends
and see one feather
falling, falling
small reminder
heartbreaks mend

Exist or Exit

Dark and oily underbelly
swirling, amorphous
motion perpetual,
unpinnable
without delineation
vortex or reference point
and in this we bleat.
I am
or am I?
while scrunching up the screaming soul
within the laced tight rigid boot
steel toed with grommets reinforced
designed to skate through
yet another day.

Atlantic Affair

A storm was brewing. One of the fishing boats had almost broken away from its mooring and was held only by a single frayed line tied to the prow. It kept tugging from side to side, back and forth like a tethered animal determined to be free. Half submerged, another boat lay in the shallows, upturned to show its rotted hull and broken ribs. It was truly dead but the floating boat kept nudging it gently in the stern and grazing along its side, a gentle foreplay which caused the rotted hull to creak and shudder.

The movements seemed too sensuous for inanimate objects and the man watched, transfixed for several moments, allowing his mind to consider the possibility that these boats were of more than just wood and nails. He snapped the thought away and kept on walking.

Farther along the road he was glad of his decision not to allow any hint of the metaphysical to taint his rationale. Old rope from the loft of a decrepit fish shed had slipped down across the lintel beam, forming the shape of an empty noose, which hung in the doorway, swinging wildly with the wind.

"Great shot! Gotta' use it… but not in this lifetime," he thought, remembering that he was no longer behind the camera.

As the road tapered off onto the beach, so did the signs of recent use. Sands washed in from winter storms disrupted his gait. Corroded locks still hung on doors of ramshackle fish sheds with roofs long gone and wharves rose and fell with every wave, floating high on the first Spring tide.

He loved the violence of a storm. It echoed the turmoil of his past emotions, a strength that had dominated his films, causing reviewers to describe them as powerful and gritty. To be young and naïve enough to believe that things, any things mattered was something. Whether curse or blessing he wasn't sure, the only certainty being that it was no longer his, this capacity to care.

It used to be that when he drank the numbness dissipated; now it only intensified, hung like webs of heavy chain, but still he drank and awoke from stupors that should have carried him through until morning to see the time winking at him, two:thirty five or three:forty two.

It would have been easier to believe that this had all begun with her death but in fact he'd had it long before to a lesser degree; the feeling of being set apart from life, observer not participant, unable to step out from behind the camera. A gangrene of the soul, she called it; claimed it was what they had in common, why they got along so well. Initially, perhaps she was right but with her, life had regained some meaning for him. He had recaptured some of his capacity for emotion and in retrospect he wondered if he had sucked the last dregs of her vitality for his own nourishment. He tore his coat open with the hope that the icy wind on his flesh might freeze these thoughts before they flourished.

The impact of the wind seem to compress his body and cause his limbs to flail outward, not forward. His eyes were half closed against the blast and unconsciously his mouth was gaping. When he realized this he closed his mouth and couldn't see as well. Consciously he opened his mouth and saw more clearly. It was a strange phenomenon and he was unable to understand why he could see more clearly with his mouth open. It wasn't that he was particularly drunk he decided but merely choosing to disregard the confines of reality, the sign of a truly flexible mind. He congratulated himself.

Waves were crashing against the rocks which protected both sides of the rocky peninsula and splashing heavily onto the path he followed.

"Give those men with buckets double pay. They're working hard tonight," he roared defiantly, only to choke on the final words and reach frantically for the bottle in his pocket. He slumped down, lowered his head, closed his mouth and clutched the coat tightly to his neck, numbed by the realization that he was reliving her emotions, doing just what she had been doing on the night they met.

She had been just so drunk and totally secure in the belief that she was alone on the peninsula, a minute splinter from the original heaven, as she described it on one of her more congenial days. The humidity had been oppressive on that hot, electric night and huge rain drops were just beginning to splatter on the rocks as he heard the first obscenities hurled out into the heavy air. She was voluble and sounded vicious and he, amused and curious, had decided to remain invisible in the darkness until she passed by. But she didn't pass by, she stopped ten, maybe fifteen feet away from him and lay down on the sand, in the rain to drink.

She was beautiful. At least to him she was beautiful but he could admit to himself that in a crowd he might not have noticed her. This caused him to question: was she truly beautiful, to be more precise desirable or was his perception distorted by his lust?

In an effort to be analytical as he continued along the shore with the freezing rain lashing his face, he allowed himself to remember the firmness of her slender thighs. They were beautiful, misleadingly girlish and in contrast to her hands which were emaciated, like birds' feet with painted talons. He always felt they shouldn't be a part of her. He remembered how they held a glass, the way the bony fingers cradled it so carefully. Without alcohol she swore she would not live and she used it like a

77

ATLANTIC AFFAIR

JENNI BLACKMORE — COUNTING CROWS

medication, measured and constantly. It often surprised him how she kept her equilibrium. No matter how much she drank there seemed to be a point of reason, a line her mind would not cross. Once, when he wanted to paddle to Australia, just the two of them in her canoe she had deemed it impossible at such a moment of drunken clarity when nothing seemed impossible to him.

From then on he hesitated to drink with her, drink for drink, for fear she would view him from a more sober vantage point. It piqued him that her capacity seemed greater than his. It shouldn't have mattered but it did. He didn't want to be laughed at. She could laugh so heartily at everyone's futility, especially her own. She often amazed him by recounting her most humiliating moments with such hilarity and detachment.

One night she described visiting three men, business partners who owned a luxury cottage close to where she lived. Her description was explicit, detailing things he didn't want to know about her. Unrestrained by conventional shames she spoke from a voyeur's perspective, describing images of herself performing as if from both sides of a two way mirror. He didn't want to hear, didn't want to see the scene she painted with her words and he interrupted her before she had finished.

"That stuff is all in the past. What's the point in reviving old ghosts from years gone by?"

"It was last week." Her voice was quiet, her head tilted slightly as she looked directly into his face, smiling at his confusion, showing her teeth which were very white and slightly translucent.

"You didn't expect that, did you? Surprise! That's what happens when you try to change the rules half way through the game. How long have we been doing this? A year almost? Me, paddling across the inlet in my little canoe to visit my clandestine lover in his rustic kingdom. You, satisfying my cravings, which are voracious but not too diverse, you must agree. Liquor and sex, that's what it was all about. Didn't need a signed contract to know that. And it was good when we could be like two white pebbles rolling around in the glass jar of our own addictions with no grubby residue of emotional needs, no promises dragging in the dust like umbilical cords needing to get severed. But it wasn't good enough for you, you bastard, you had to crack the godamn jar with your 'love' talk and your 'let's-make-this-work-baby' crap.

The man crumpled to his knees in much the same way he had done on that final night when she'd said those words to him. Rolling over he pillowed his head against a rock. He was more drunk than he'd realized as he began to replay his reel of memory; last scene, act one.

"What the hell do you want out of life anyway?" he shouts, tightening his grip on her arm.

"I want to do whatever I please. Preferably without some fucking do-gooder asking me what I want out of life." She turns and glares at him with angry disdain.

"Can't you understand there has to be an end?" He releases her arm and his falls limply by his side as his anger drains, leaving only pain.

"Of course there has to be an end. From the moment we are born it keeps creeping closer to us. That's what I want out of life. I want it to be over."

She sweeps her hand in front of her with a gesture of finality. He grabs it, this time more firmly than before.

"You're hurting my arm." Her jaw is clenched, her words come quiet and clipped.

He pulls her roughly towards him. He can smell her body; the whiskey, the expensive perfume, her sex and tobacco.

"If you don't let me go I'll knee you in the balls, if I can find them that is." She turns away and glares impatiently at the wall, waiting to be released.

"Just tell me why", he begs.

Once again she looks at him directly and begins to tell him why. She tells him about her husband, a public figure, rich and respected and about her two daughters, pre-adolescents with hair like silk and pale, pale skin. She describes how her husband encouraged her reliance on alcohol, ever ready to re-stock the bar, to re-fill her glass; to designate Mondays as her special day to lay in bed with a bottle and a book, doors locked, phones unplugged, while he looked after the girls.

"He's very smooth", she explains. "He's very persuasive. For him it's easy to make the obscene acceptable, to make defilement seem desirable. It's his knack, his special gift."

She has become very calm. The man senses the ether of her pain as it spreads. He can see the colour of the couch they sit on. It is green. It is leather. He remembers choosing it but all other thought is obliterated by her words. The haze of alcohol has vanished. The moment cracks with crystal clarity.

"Every night I used to brush my daughters' hair before they went to bed. It was a ritual, my way of loving them, until one night my youngest daughter took the brush and knelt between her father's knees in a posture of absolute submission. He lowered the paper he was reading and pulled his glasses a little way from his eyes before he gave me one small smile. In that instant I understood exactly what had been going on. I looked across at my other daughter. She looked smug, she looked like she was challenging me: *go on, I dare you to accuse him.* They were all looking at me like that. The child was still kneeling with her head between her father's knees and he was slowly fondling a lock of her hair. He smiled again, very slowly and said, "Perhaps you should have another drink".

The rain was icy as it trickled across the man's face and down his neck but he remembered only the oppressive heat of the morning: last scene, last act.

The fog is hanging like a curtain along the water-line. It is thick and opaque, yet the sun's rays burn the salt onto his back and give him a shadow as he walks along, as if to assure him of his existence. At the same time foaming tongues suck away his footprints, destroying any evidence of his presence. This conflict echoes his inner turmoil as he drags his toenails in the wet sand.

He needs to see her again. He needs the time to convince her that it can be worked out. The girls can be taken from their father, they can all go to counselling, he will stop drinking and she can... A lone seagull, invisible in the fog, screams abuse somewhere above him and in the distance he hears a dog bark and children shouting from the farthest tip of the peninsula.

By the time he reaches the action a black car is sloughing through the dunes and someone has covered her body with a gaudy beach towel. Her hair is dragged out behind, still touched by every seventh wave and one leg is bent upwards at the knee. Her skinny arm with its claw-like hand stretches out towards him.

An elegant man in a dark suit leaves the car and walks decisively towards the body on the beach, followed by two young girls with flowing blond hair.

As his reel of memory sputtered to an end the drunken man allowed his head to slide down off the rock and he shifted his body into the same position hers had been in when he saw it for the last time. Back at his house a voice on the radio was announcing that the freezing rain warnings would be continued.

The Gift

It truly was the most memorable of Christmas Eves.

"I work until noon," she had said.

"If necessary the appointment can be at twelve forty-five."

The doctor's receptionist was being so beautifully human, wanting to leave early yet not wanting to refuse the woman.

"If you can get here any earlier we'd appreciate it. And the reason for your visit?"

"It's just a skin lesion. The doctor wanted to see it, if it ever happened again."

"A rash you say?"

"Yes, a rash. I'll be there as early as I can."

She left her office at eleven and was in the examining room by twelve.

He was a wonderful doctor, still fresh enough to be idealistic. He had a compassionate smile which seemed to indicate that he really did care. She couldn't look at him directly, fearing she was already too close to tears, so instead her eyes strayed towards the diagram of an infected lung taped to the wall behind his head.

"Do you remember how we discussed the possibility of me being infected with genital herpes? Since then the conversation has always bothered me and now I have a minor sore spot, like the one I had before. I'm sure it's nothing serious but I just wanted you to put my mind at rest. Perhaps so it doesn't seem like I'm

wasting your time altogether I could get a pap smear taken
at the same time and then it will seem like there is a reason for
this visit. It's so very slight, the sore spot, that I feel embarrassed
to be wasting your time, especially on Christmas Eve. I just need
you to put my mind at rest.

"I'm glad you came. That was a wise decision. Strip from the waist
down and use this."

The doctor handed her a paper sheet.

She lay on the examining table, effectively naked, with her legs
together, covered by the paper sheet. Not wanting to anticipate the
humiliation of, 'slide down please, feet in the stirrups' she stared
instead at the vibrating ceiling light and considered the other
problems in her life. There was her loneliness to think of and her
melancholy, the emptiness she tried to subdue with alcohol and
her warring daughters who showed no signs of recovering from
the trauma of their early childhood. In comparison, the dis-
comfort of her present situation was negligible, she told her-
self. She could handle it.

The doctor entered and began to peel on his protective
gloves but he didn't touch her. Instead he asked, "Do you
know that you have two wonderful daughters? The last
time they were here I couldn't help comparing them
with other girls their age. They do seem to be inordi-
nately smart and very pretty too."

She nodded her head, affirmative and wondered silent-   85
ly, "Why is he telling me this?"

"And your sister; it seems I am seeing her face more in
the newspapers than in my office these days. She's doing
very well for herself."

"Yes, she's becoming quite well known."

THE GIFT

"Are you close to her?"

"Yes, I suppose, quite close. We didn't used to be, as kids and especially not when I was married; she hated him, but now she's very kind to the girls and we have our good moments."

There was a pause, he seemed to know that there was still much left unsaid. The doctor waited attentively.

"It was always difficult for me to accept her sexuality, well, you understand she never made much of an effort to hide the fact that she was gay. It's not such a big deal now but it was hell for me going through high school three years after she did, so I blamed her for a lot of stuff I probably shouldn't have. But things are better now. There's still a certain amount of forgiving that needs to be done but yes, I guess you could say we are fairly close."

The woman lay, wishing he'd be done. Any talk of closeness or emotion brought her close to tears and she preferred to avoid it. She just wanted him to examine her so she could be gone but still he stood there.

"You're quite a lucky woman when you think of it. You escaped a horrendous situation that many women never get out of. They spend the rest of their lives married to monsters, no better than the man who was your husband. You still have the best part of your life ahead of you and you're very attractive. I saw you a couple of weeks ago walking down the road with one of your daughters. Even from a distance I thought, 'what an attractive woman' and as I drove closer you became even more attractive. It was then that I recognized you. I'm just an average guy and I'm happily married, so considering my reaction, do you have any idea how many men are looking at you and wanting to know you better and not every man's a monster, you know."

She felt very vulnerable as she lay on the table unable to meet his eyes, staring instead at his gloved hands.

Why is he talking to me this way? How does he know how badly I'm feeling? Is it written all over me in large neon letters, SORROW, HEARTACHE, EMPTINESS? Is that what everyone sees when they look at me?

The doctor gazed down at the woman under the paper sheet.

"Yes," he continued, "soon you will meet someone who will love you in the way you deserve to be loved. I know this will happen. Do you believe me?"

It was such a direct question. She couldn't respond to a pair of surgical gloves. Forcing her eyes to travel upwards until they reached his chin she nodded and silently mouthed the word 'yes'.

He was a doctor. He was trying to make her feel better. That was why he was saying these things and it horrified her. If he could sense the depth of her melancholy enough to perceive it as something that needed curing, then the melancholy was indeed very real and not as volatile as she had tried to believe. The fact of whether or not she had herpes was no longer the issue. It was a much more painful and virulent virus he was treating.

The ceiling lights were humming quietly. The doctor flexed his rubberized fingers.

"A pap smear. It's always a good idea, especially at your age. How old are you? Forty one? That's incredible. If I didn't know I would guess twenty seven. You seem so young. Slide down please. Any other problems? Anything I need to know?"

Many things. You need to know how married woman sense me as a threat and avoid me; you need to know how their husbands see me as a toy, part of the game they play to re-vitalize their sagging masculinity; you need to know how my sister's friends all see me as a natural convert. You need to know what it's like to feel confused and defensive in the company of men and women, to avoid a woman's kiss, her secretive touch, to conceal a man's advances for the sake of his wife, your friend. There are many things you need to know, she thought as she replied quietly, "No there's nothing".

Carefully he removed the instrument from her vagina saying, "Well, everything looks fine around the cervix. It is genital herpes."

He spoke them and disowned them. The words floated like raucous crows in the white room.

"You didn't look carefully enough. I'm sure you must be wrong."

The doctor shook his head. She pressed the palms of her hands against her eyes as tears slid down across her cheek bones, dampening her hair.

"Get dressed. I'll be back to talk to you."

The tears stopped. She felt numb, a dry socket.

It's better if you bleed, she thought as she pulled the velvet pants over her thighs and slipped on the patent shoes. Her festive clothes seemed suddenly absurd and quietly she murmured, "Merry Fucking Christmas! To the girl who has everything. Great kids, wonderful sister, incredible looks, talent and... herpes."

Since she had been divorced, since the never-ending struggle of making it through each storm filled day and lonely night had begun; sometime since then, someone had told her that she had broad shoulders, that she could take it. Sitting on the plastic chair, leaning her head against the diseased lung poster, she sobbed dryly and wondered just how broad her shoulders would need to be.

As the doctor re-entered the room he was definite.

"You must not let this upset you in such a way. It's not life threatening or particularly serious, you must keep things in proportion."

"Is there no chance that you could be mistaken?"

For the first time she stared directly at him and the hurt in her eyes unsettled him. He shook his head slowly. She shook her head also.

"I can't believe it. If I'd been sleeping around, well fine, but I slept with the same man for fifteen years. He was the one and only person in my life. There has been no-one since. Do you understand? I haven't slept with anyone else but now you're telling me that I am diseased."

"You are not diseased. Don't ever say that. You have a virus. It's just like a cold sore that comes in a different place."

The woman sobbed and shook her head, blond hair falling across her hands as they covered her face.

"No. It's not the same. Don't try to tell me it's the same as a cold sore!"

"Anna, you have to believe me. It's not that bad. You can still live a perfectly normal life."

"I am diseased. I am contaminated. I have a sleazy virus living in my body and you're trying to tell me that I can still live a normal life?"

"You have to believe me."

"I can't believe you. I can't. I can't believe that one man would be allowed to take so many privileges. He wasted fifteen years of my life. He destroyed my children. He crushed my soul. I thought I was finally rid of him and now you're telling me that he planted a virus that will stay with me forever. You must be mistaken?"

The doctor shook his head. A safety valve released within the woman and suddenly she felt light headed.

"It's a perfect Christmas gift for the girl who has everything, isn't it?" She laughed. "He would love the irony of it all. At least I can deprive him of that and if it happens that I do get the chance to dance on his grave I'll certainly take a few extra steps in memory of this moment. I don't supposed it shocks to know that I would love to see him dead, after all he did to me, after all he did to the girls. I even tried to kill him once myself. It was close to Christmas, four? I guess five years ago now. I'd come home from work to find the girls already in bed and crying. At the time I thought it was because of the Christmas tree he'd thrown out the door. I had not yet even begun to imagine what else he was capable of and of course the girls were too scared to tell me. He was very drunk and that was when he was most dangerous so all I could do was sit, waiting for him to pass out. He tried to go to the bathroom but fell and couldn't get up so he urinated on the kitchen floor. This was vastly amusing to him and it was at this moment that my desire to kill him became overwhelming.

There was a medication in the house, I'm sure you're familiar with it. It's supposed to stop drunks from drinking by creating in them a violent reaction to alcohol. Previously, on a couple of occasions when I'd tried to leave, he'd promised to change. He'd stood in front of me and taken this medication. Of course, he'd merely hidden it under his tongue and spit it out again but I didn't know that at the time, only when he laughed about it later when telling me just how stupid I was. There was a warning on the container; it could be lethal if mixed with alcohol because the reaction was so severe. I took several of the capsules and sprinkled the contents into some mustard which I then spread on a ham sandwich. He'd passed out by this time and I knew that when he came to he'd stagger into the kitchen and find the sandwich where I'd left it on the counter. He's a greedy man and I knew he'd eat it when he saw it and I truly believed that it would kill him. I imagined him writhing in agony on the floor, right where he'd peed and I fell to sleep on the couch, feeling more peace than I'd felt in several years but for some reason I woke up around four a.m. and put the sandwich in the garbage. This is one of many moments that I've regretted doing that."

The doctor's eyes welled with sympathy and the woman thought that he would need to develop at least a little cynicism to temper the overload of his patients' anguish.

Later that day as she drove out of the shopping centre with the back seat loaded with last minute buys, a car with three men in stopped to let her through. She smiled and waved, acknowledging their courtesy and they all waved back enthusiastically. They looked young and had apparently already begun to celebrate. At the first stop light they pulled in front of her and the man in the back seat turned and smiled again. He looked to be healthy and uncomplicated. She smiled at him and laughed bitterly to herself.

"Fool! You have no idea what you would be getting yourself into."

She spoke the words out loud to herself and the sound of her voice emphasized the quietness in the car. She turned the radio on and let the music reach inside her. She wound down the window to feel the cold air sting her face as it sucked out long strands of her hair. Feeling strangely elated she shifted the car, staying close behind the three men as they careened through the city.

"It's easy to flirt. Believe me, it's easy for you to have a man. Any man would want you." The doctor had said this. "And you must get a man. You must have a lover. It isn't good for you, it is normal for you to be always alone. When you see a man who is attractive to you, go to bed with him. Don't keep living in the past."

He's right, she thought. *It is easy.* And she wondered if there would be any consolation in contaminating the man in the back seat of the other car. She even wondered briefly if there would be more consolation to be gained by infecting several men that night.

The man in the car ahead kept turning and smiling at her but now more seriously, more meaningfully. He looked handsome from what she could see and she decided that he must have had many lovers already. Perhaps he already had herpes, she thought and remembered the packet of condoms in her purse. The doctor had insisted she bought some with her medication and used them when she found a lover; to protect herself from disease. He hadn't been joking. He had been perfectly serious. She wondered how she would ask the stranger to wear the condom as she handed it to him.

She heard again the doctor's words as he handed her the paper sheet, "Strip from the waist and use this."

"Is that how you do it?" She chuckled and felt invulnerable, momentarily shielded by bitterness and anger.

The sky was darkening, manganese through cobalt as the two cars raced across the bridge towards the business section. The office towers loomed black and silent across the harbour but she knew that the frenetic revelry was well underway in the trendy singles bars. The man in the car ahead was no more than a silhouette when, mid-span, the yearly phenomenon occurred. The sky had darkened enough for the first star to appear. It was indeed Christmas Eve.

Her plans changed as suddenly as they had formed .

"It's my gift," she shrugged. "Not his." And as they left the bridge she veered abruptly to the right giving only a final, brief glimpse of her tail lights to stranger in the other car.

She headed home to wrap presents and prepare her daughters for Christmas at their aunt's house. The aunt's partner blamed the current, patriarchal society for the destruction of Christmas and in protest there would be no turkey for dinner. On Christmas Day they were to dine on baked salmon. The woman wondered if gift giving would be appropriate.

Unrequited Love

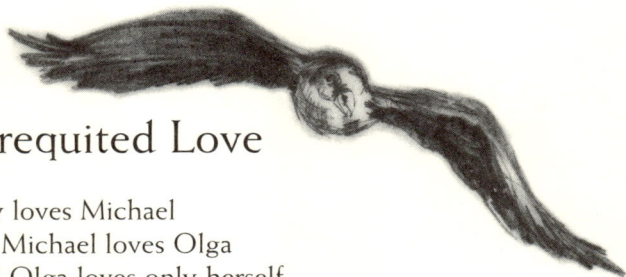

Amy loves Michael
but Michael loves Olga
and Olga loves only herself
The world is full
of unrequited love

It spirals down
like falling leaves
and blusters in
on Summer's breeze
and piles all debris
of the hurt
in every corner of a heart
It's unrequited love

It's unrequited love
It's in the stare
of vacant eyes
responsible for
aimless lives
and cruelty
from frustration born
It's unrequited love

It's everywhere
It floats like spores
and seems to spread
like canker sores
For man, for woman
for parent, for friend
it's everywhere
until the end
It's unrequited love

JENNI BLACKMORE — COUNTING CROWS

A Blizzard of Angel Feathers

Between a rock, du-du-du and a hard place!

Between a rock, der-der and a hard place!

The sounds are amplified into tangible vibrations, sinews of sound that lash out; loops, coils of raw noise that tangle around and tug the man towards the beer tent.

Sweat is running down her forehead and into one eye as she leans back for the final finale, the final lurch forward towards the mic', final flourish of fingers fighting keys. She blinks away the sweat bead and catches sight of the solitary man standing in the doorway, nothing more than another cut-out dark space.

Final song, final set and all that's left is the residue of smoke, scattered ashes on deserted tables and a littering of plastic cups that spill their dregs as the midnight wind brings in the fog.

The crowd has straggled off taking her sweater with it and she shivers. The burly waiter with the steroid pumping neck confirms it — He ain't seen no sweater — and this is when the man with the melancholy face and the garbage bag under his arm asks her if she wants to buy a T-shirt. If there are lower than low places, places wedged between the toughest rocks and the meanest of hard places, for her this feels like one of them. She knows before looking that the shirts will have pictures of tall masted ships lurching across the front of them and the labels removed from the back seam, just to confirm their inferior quality.

95

"You wanna' buy a T-shirt?" Even as the words spring-board from his tongue he knows their dive is doomed.

"Do I want to what?" She doesn't need to call him roach-head, her tone says it all.

"I'm sorry. I've been saying that all day. You can have one... I mean please take one. There's only a few left and after tonight no one's going to... well I don't imagine...

The waiter is stacking chairs with brutal efficiency.

"Closin", he grunts above the racket he's creating. "Bar's closed."

The man looks over his shoulder, assessing the empty space surrounding the chair he sits on. In one corner a couple huddle together against the red vinyl wall of the tent, oblivious to all but the subterranean language of love which absorbs them.

The barman follows his gaze and walks toward the lovers. The piano player also turns to leave and for whatever reason the solitary man can't stop himself from blurting out, "Parade of Sail — short sleeved or long, take your pick. I don't have any sweat-shirts left but a T-shirt would be better than nothing".

"I think I'd rather be seen dead, thanks just the same."

Her skin already has a sallow cast and the flesh of her cheeks is slightly drawn by the constant effort of keeping her lips pulled together over protruding teeth. The man thinks she must surely snore when she sleeps on her back but this is fine with him. He does not want to see her sleeping, he does not want to see her dead, he just wants to be rid of the T-shirts and as he stands, before he disappears into the fog, he shoves the garbage bag to the end of the table.

"Help yourself if you change your mind. They're no good to me anymore."

Have you ever been walking on the waterfront in Halifax?
Have you ever been walking on the waterfront in Halifax at
midnight in the fog with a run in your tights, just wishing you
could spot the creep who stole your sweater?

There's a feeling that comes with the end of a gig; a drained, done
over kind of feeling that seems like it won't ever leave. Bad gigs,
gigs when everyone talks and nobody listens and nobody cares that
you're singing your soul away; bad gigs make that drained out feel-
ing real hard to shake so you flop onto a bench and stare into the
night because a.) it doesn't seem like you've got the energy to walk
any farther and b.) it doesn't seem to matter much if you get
mugged; seems like it might break the monotony of draggin' arse
backwards to the hole in the wall called 'bachelor suite' complete
with stench of cat dung and forgotten garbage.

———————

There's a lonely woman sitting in the Halifax fog at midnight,
wishing she wasn't wearing black tights in the Summer.

She watches the feet of a couple wandering by. The feet are
dressed in very white sneakers and very white socks with
tops that are folded uniformly. The bright newness of it all
makes her think they must be newly married feet, newly
married honeymooning feet. For her there has never
been a honeymoon but many beginnings to aborted
journeys, accompanied by the kind of passion that pre-
cludes precise adjustment of sock tops.

The woman forcibly removes her gaze and re-focuses
on her own black tights. There's a hole at the knee
where she snagged it on the keyboard stand. For five
nights the same place, the same loose screw and differ-
ent tights, every night a different pair of tights thrown at
the trash across her room. She attempts a mental calcula-
tion of what that loose screw cost her.

A BLIZZARD OF ANGEL FEATHERS

Need to keep receipts. Need to keep a tally of this stuff. Need to keep a check on where the money goes... The big wave begins to gather and she knows its going to pull her under if she doesn't keep these thoughts at bay. H.A.L.T. She spells the word out loud. Hungry. Angry. Lonely. Tired. These are danger zones. The triteness of it all still annoys her but she knows the formula can work. She knows that she will probably feel better with food, with sleep, with company... The anger she still clings to. The anger is hers. She's not ready, doesn't think she ever will be ready to give it up.

There's a lonely man sitting in the Halifax fog at midnight. He is watching the honeymooners walk by and slowly submerging himself in a faded, well worn scene where he is the new husband watching his wife undress her feet. Much of her is blurred by the visual distancing of time but he still sees clearly her delicate ankle and the high arching instep of the feet he had chosen to lay his soul out for. It is the feel of her toes, no coarser than the surface of his tongue as he licks them; it is the memory of this texture that causes the abrasion, that scratches at his deepest wounds until they bleed again.

At this certain point of despair, when the draining has left an emptiness that sucks in on itself like a vacuum and causes a gut ache that is distinctly physical, the man wishes his kid was home. If the boy was home the man knows he could construct a purpose for what he might do next but the boy is staying with his grandmother so the man remains seated in the fog.

"Still trying to sell T-shirts?"

He smiles weakly, briefly and sinks back into his reverie before she has walked by him. She regrets her tone instantly and tries to neutralize it by saying, "Thanks for the offer, just the same."

His lack of response causes her to try harder. "If it was food you'd been giving, now that would have been different. I'd have been right in there with both hands and a doggy bag."

The man glances up, realizing she is still there and talking to him. Her words have not entered his conciousness and he reaches for them, arranging them for meaning like magnetic letters on a metal board.

"Food? Yeah, well guess not, huh?" he mumbles as reply.

It's not his words that stop her. It's the place they come from. A low place; a place so low, where even the art of simple communication is above, unreachable.

"Are you hungry?" Her words, like a bug that won't be brushed away.

"Hungry?" He asks himself out loud. "No. Not really... but maybe, yes. Yes," he decides, "I'm hungry. Did you want to get something to eat?" His question seems to beg a negative response.

"Sure. It's hard for me to walk into a place, alone, at this time of night and dressed in my stage clothes. Gives the wrong impression you know." And as they walk she continues to herself — *and so I pick up a guy on the water-front and get him to buy me food. What kind of impression does that give?*

She is sensitive about impressions. After years of counselling and group therapy there's not too much that does not get carefully analyzed. She knows how this will go down at the next meeting. Everyone will say it's a typical example of how 'survivors' go looking for abuse because that's all they know. The group thinks she goes out of her way to be a victim. Someone will probably ask if he reminded her of her father and is that why she picked him up and she formulates her reply as they walk in silence through the fog.

At the next meeting the group listens attentively. "I picked him up because there's a certain camaraderie between workers at festivals. The transience of their situation speeds up the friendship process. If it don't happen quick, it don't happen. It's okay for you people who work the same job for years, see the same people; gigs last for days not years so the dynamic is different."

"Bullshit!" The woman who responds is new to the group. She badly needs what they can give but the group is thinking how it doesn't need this wild woman with the rawness of her pain always lashing out to inflict. The piano player is insensed by this interruption and breathes rapidly. Her lips are clamped down tightly over her protruding teeth which sometimes are mistaken for the semblance of a smile but not at this moment. She does not continue. She does not describe the weary slices of pizza she eats with the melancholy man or the slices of their weary lives, chewed over with olives and peppers and bacon.

Compared with hers his pain is pretty bland as she remembers it; a vegetarian, without the works. So the wife died and it broke his heart; he still has his kid and a house and stuff going for him, just needs to stop being a bottom feeder and rise to the surface again, she had thought as he served up his life, slice by slice.

Her anger cools and her attention returns to the group. They are discussing friendships. Can they exist between men and women, without sex. It seems to be the theory of choice and someone suggests that all people, but especially survivors, should be friends for months, years even before they consider becoming lovers.

"Bullshit!" The newcomer is off again and the meeting rapidly dissolves.

Later the man asks, "How was the meeting?"

"Not great," she responds. "Not great at all. I got accused of picking you up because I lust after abuse and no one was able to convincingly demonstrate that friendship can exist between the sexes without the usual complications, so right now I'm wondering why I waste my time going."

"My mother went to meetings for years and years. Meetings were the part of her life that kept the rest of it together, is what she used to say."

The piano player wants to know why the mother went to meetings and the man tells her a typical story about a woman who marries an alcoholic and remains as a wife too long. Too much time goes by before she crawls away, and she's unable to remember who she really is. Going to meetings seems to help and so she goes and keeps on going; the meetings become her dependency, her addiction. Her spirit develops a miraculous elasticity, like some eternal bungie jumper, bouncing up and down and up and up but never quite high enough, never quite able to make it back to the original plateau.

One winter night, black and bitter she pulls into the semi-deserted parking lot alongside the regular cars, some with stickers suggesting that life be lived by the day, others claiming the friendship of Bill W. The mother is outside, locking her car when a white feather comes spiralling down out of nowhere and lands on the car door by her hand. There are no birds flying above, it is the dead of winter, dead of night. There are no trees, no nests. She looks at the feather for several moments and she hears a voice telling her to take it, to keep it and she can see the arching underside of a giant wing and she knows exactly where the feather came from and she stops going to meetings and continues to live happily.

The piano player askes the man what the feather looked like.

"You asked about my mother going to meetings. I shouldn't have mentioned the feather. She believes that with an angel watching out for her she's got nothing to worry about. Maybe it's true. Since the feather she's the most together lady I know. Or maybe she's crazy but she doesn't drink anymore and she's happy, all because she keeps a feather tucked away in a velvet pouch she keeps in her bedroom."

"So what's it look like?" The piano player is becoming impatient.

The man is reticent. He does not want to admit that he has not seen the feather and does not want to see the feather. She is needling him now, suggesting that he does not want to confront the issue. He displays more passion than she thought him capable of as he retorts angrily,

"My mother can have her angel feather. My son can look at it any time he wants to but it would take more than a feather to change my life. I had my dream and now it's gone. There's nothing more I want to say about feathers."

It is the unspoken words that cause the piano player to move towards the man, the man who tells the story of his mother's life as if he had never been more than an observer. It is the first time they have embraced and as the woman takes him gently in her

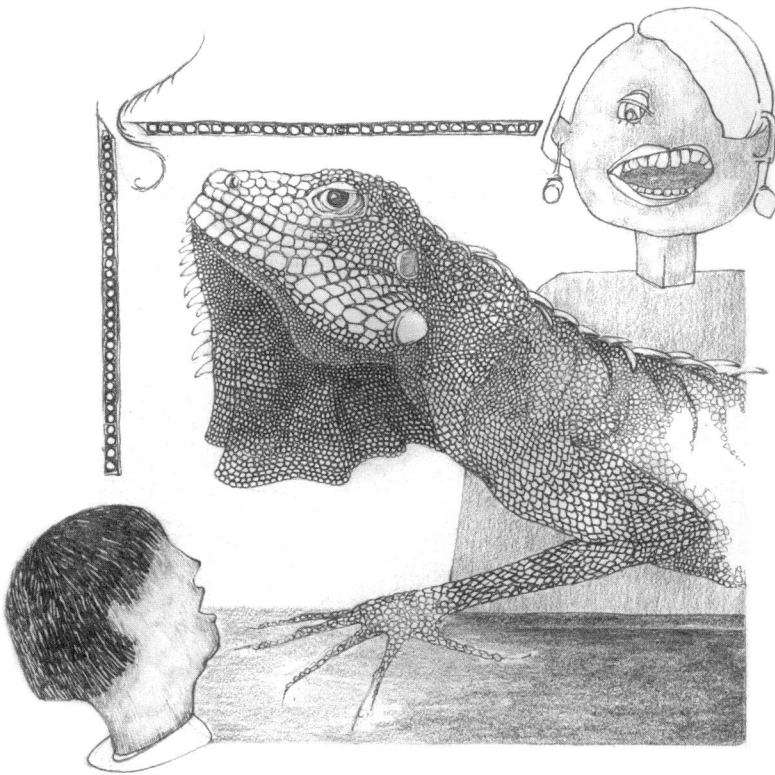

arms she feels the starkness of his ribs, the resistance in
his shoulders and the first shudder of grief, finally will-
ing to be set free.

The man's son is not pleased when the piano player
moves into their house. The boy is squat, stolid and
intense. The woman thinks she would find him difficult
to like, even under optimum conditions. She is relieved
that he chooses to ignore her and after a couple of pre-
posterous attempts at mothering, she graciously abandons
the role. With all the complex reasoning of an adolescent

A BLIZZARD OF ANGEL FEATHERS

who has deified a mother he can no longer remember, the son wages war, using guilt and self pity as his primary weapons.

He has a pet lizard, almost three feet long which has the run of the house. Pets reflect their owners: the lizard supports this hypothesis. It responds negatively or not at all and usually remains motionless, often unobserved, watching with an unwavering eye. When it does react to any stimuli it's on the defensive, reared to full height, dewlap displayed and darkened with anger. It's rough and cold to the touch, awkward and ungainly, yet swift and painfully accurate with it's lashing tail.

The piano player has been working as a waitress. Her feet hurt and she's dog tired as she flops into the chair. She does not notice the lizard, draped across the seat like a scaly boa. As she leaps up and forwards she trips on some school work scattered across the floor and finds herself looking up at the boy who is screaming incoherently and waving his arms towards the lizard which is attempting to skitter off with a lop-sided and less than agile gait.

The woman's head is beginning throb where she knocked it against something on the way down and her feet still hurt even though she is no longer standing on them. There is a momentary pause before the boy begins swiping books onto the floor in a frantic attempt to retrieve the traumatized lizard which has crawled in behind the bookshelf.

"Get those god-damn books back on the shelf," she screams, still prone but now propped on one elbow. "And these too!" 'Elementary Science for the Classroom' and 'Mathematics for Today' are launched on a flight path towards the boy. 'Elementary Science" hits him on the ankle and he begins to howl inordinately, balancing on one leg.

"And take that... and that... and that... " The woman continues to hurl books across the room; 'Whole Language Learning', 'Our Society Today' and a binder that breaks open as it hits the bookcase and scatters sheets of scribble at the boy's feet.

"That's it! That's my fucking homework. Now I won't fucking well grade. Thanks a lot BABE. Just thanks a fucking big pile!" The boy kicks the binder back at the woman.

"You shit!" she screams, "You little shit. Just let me get... " She attempts to stand but it's her ankle now as well as her feet and her head that hurts. She grabs onto the chair for support and snatches up a pillow, needing something to throw.

"Oh, no! I'm really scared now", mocks the boy, allowing his resentment to flow freely. "Oh, please don't hit me with that scary pillow, nice lady. Here, let me protect myself." The boy snatches a pillow off the couch and instantly they are fighting with all the insanity of unrestrained anger, venting months of subjugated rage to feed the fury of this spontaneous combustion. There are no holds barred, it is a pillow fight to the death.

It's a pillow that succumbs first. Bleeding a few feathers initially and then a few more until the combatants stop to take notice. It is the boy's weapon which has split. He hits the woman with it, this time not to hurt her but just to see the feathers fly. His face is contorted, confused, wondering whether it should smile or not.

105

"Here, let me try," demands the woman as she snatches the remains of the pillow from him. "I thought this only happened in movies."

"You mean pillow fights with real feathers?" questions the boy.

"I'm not sure," replies the woman.

She has just heard a strange sound that echoes in a place of distant memory. It is the sound of her own laughter, spontaneous and truly joyful.

The man has appeared. He stands in the doorway, surveying the debris, wondering how much more of this incendiary turmoil he can endure.

"What the hell… ?" he begins wearily.

"A blizzard," explains the boy, with an unexpected smile.

"Angels feathers, I think," the woman concurs.

Living in a State of Grace

Confucius, you were wrong. Wrong! Confucius... YOU... were... WRONG. I savour the words like silky-soft candy, rolling them around inside my mouth, across my tongue. Self indulgent? You bet! And when I become bored with the sound of my own voice I assume a new persona, affect a different enunciation: a ruthless Russian spy; a sexy Swedish starlet; Her Royal Highness; Elmer Fudd.

"Confucius, you were wrong," they say, with my permission. What a glorious copyright, and it is mine.

Confucius, there is a State of Grace, I know because I have lived there. Your mistrust of the twenty second configuration in the ancient Book of Changes was invalid. When you threw the yarrow sticks, when they indicated fire from the secret depths of earth, blazing to illuminate the mountain, heavenly heights, you should have trusted their message, should have allowed yourself to live in the State of Grace, enjoying its tranquil beauty: clarity within, quiet without, pure moments in a capsule of gentle time, unaffected by the past and without influence on the future.

Imagine a feather falling, slow motion, dreamscape, spiralling slowly, never landing; this is the State of Grace. Nothing really counts. Nothing really stops but neither do things progress. It's a suspension, this State of Grace, a bubble which does not burst when poked.

See me, inside the bubble, little woman with big problems and see him, as he stands at my door displaying all the fashion sense of a retired sausage vendor. I never did like satin ball-jackets. His is blue. I can't look at him too closely, or is it that I can't see him clearly beneath the brim of his ball-cap? or is it that I'm not able to compute the fifty year-old eyes, the thirty year-old smile, the boy-

ish black curls and the fake tan into one cognizant image.
I search for a clue, a defining feature that tells what the man
is. A failure! The words, shunted forward from the archives
of some past dismay, categorize this mixture of absurdi-
ties, shovelled onto my doorstep, wearing satin and
sneakers in the snow.

See the capsule enlarge. I am cooking. He is eating. We
don't talk of past or future. We don't discuss love or
money. We savour yams in stir-fry. I ask him a person-
al question — Does he like yams in stir-fry? He pre-
tends to, while wishing for fries and fat meat.

Contrary to popular opinion, I'm not such a bad guy. To
further set the record straight, I drink because I like to,
not because I have to and yes, sometimes I do drugs but
not always.

Darrell Bonang tells everyone he'll kill me if I go near his
daughter. What Darrell doesn't know is that I'd have to take a
number if I wanted to even get close; just a typical example of
how it's all in the perception and not necessarily in the reality of
the situation, when it comes to chicks.

In my experience chicks get what they ask for and then pretend it's
not what they want. Maybe the odd one is really naïve and believes
it when you say you love them, but for the most part they know
what's what. They can talk the talk just as good as any guy when it
comes right down to it and some of them even better. Dunphie's
wife for instance, she's a riot when she gets going. Myself, I don't
get off on women who come on that strong but sometimes I'll play
along just for laughs.

I was at Herbie Newan's a couple of weeks ago and everyone's
drinking the stuff he brews up, like they were connoisseurs or

something, starting out so polite, saying how good it tastes and how they'll just have one small drink before they leave, etcetera and before you know it they are out of it, big time. Talk about screwed up synapses! Nothing connects and the conversation just keeps getting weirder and weirder. Just another typical Saturday night around here, except for a guy I hadn't seen before who could really make Newan's old guitar sing. He helped cut down on the boredom quota some.

Dunphie's wife was there with a big case of the hots for this new guy. I've never seen a woman who can find as many excuses to stick some part of her anatomy in your face as Dunphie's wife can. If she's not bending over to pick something up, she's reaching across the table and giving the word 'cleavage' a whole new dimension and Dunphie, well he's always so far out of it that he doesn't even notice what goes on.

I'm just sitting back sipping on a beer, enjoying the show and the new guy, he's not drinking anything so when the shine monkeys start going off to their own little planets him and me are the only ones still talking the same language. He's starting to get real tired of Dunphie's wife, which is not surprising, especially when she takes to calling him 'The Rod' instead of Rodney, which is his name, even though it doesn't suit him one bit. I'm thinking she should call him Rod-riguez because of the fake tan he's gone too heavy on. Like why would a guy use fake tan? And if you gotta' use it at least get it on straight, for God's sake! He's got a streak down one cheek that you can't help but notice. So, the fake tan doesn't do a thing for me but otherwise 'The Rod' seems okay and like I say, he can really play guitar.

We decide to split when Newan and Blanchard start arguing over whose old dog sired the most pups. I just know it'll be all down hill from there on in and I don't want to be there when the police arrive because I'm under age and already on probation. 'The Rod' seems equally anxious to leave before Dunphie's wife rapes him so we end up walking down the road together. Naturally we get talking about how obnoxious woman can get when they're drunk and he's soon telling me stories that are hard to believe about when he played piano in the Miami Beach bars, which seems like it must have been about all his life according to all the experiences he had.

We're having a good laugh as we're walking along but there's things I'm trying to figure about the guy. Like how old he is. Thirty? Forty? Fifty? He looks like thirty but I know he's got to be older because he mentions his kid who's eighteen, (says he looks a lot like me) which makes me think that Rodney's got to be over forty but less than fifty. So what's a guy of his age, who could be playing piano in a Florida bar doing walking down the Harbour Road, Nova Scotia in the middle of winter wearing a blue silk ball jacket and a fake tan? Maybe he had to leave town in a hurry; I could understand that with all the women he's been mixed up with. Or maybe he's just out of rehab' or jail. That would explain the 'Kwik Tan'.

Anyway, we're having a good laugh, walking along and forgetting about how many miles there is to go until we come to my turn off and he still keeps walking along with me and he says,

"Hey! so you live down here too?"

and this is when I get spooked and say,

"Hey yourself. I'm the one who lives down here. Where the hell are you going?"

Well he's sort of staying with his uncle, he tells me, except that the uncle's girl friend is going wacky and keeps putting his things out in the snow, so he's thinking of moving into the house next door with some woman and her two kids.

Now it's not hard to figure out who the uncle is because there's only seven houses on our road so that leaves no doubt as to who the woman is. We both clue in at the same moment and things get really quiet and all you can hear is the scrunching of snow as we walk along. I just know he's going over every single thing he's said that night, wondering if he blew his cover and I get this sick gut feeling and I know just what Darrell Bonang feels like when I say,

"You touch my mother and I'll kill you".

————

We have snow this year. Good dry snow that stays white and sparkles in the sun. Against the brightness his blue jacket contrasts clearly as he waits for me to walk with him. We walk and talk for miles, for days, always on the periphery, carefully describing a circle that skirts the thin ice of intimacy and touches nothing but the continuation of itself. We are a man and a woman, dark shapes isolated against the whiteness, together yet separate.

A borrowed keyboard moves in before he does, and fills the void of silence in the house. Music is his gift and his fingers wander with endless melodies even when his mind is elsewhere. He tells me nothing of these places and I keep my problems as my own but we are friends and as the days progress we become inseparable. He asks for nothing and I accept only his music and his presence. With no requirements and no expectations there are no disappointments. It is a state of grace, of beauty with no fathoming for the future, no apologies for the past.

My boys resent this intrusion. They guard me fiercely, sniff the air like dogs, watch silently, always searching for a single sign and warning,

"If he touches you we'll kill him".

For once they are wise. They know this man with too
much past and not enough future cannot fill the irregular
space in our family puzzle. Sometimes however, when
we all eat together, the food seems to gain an added
vibrancy of colour, taste and smell; there is laughter
with his music, warmth and crackle from the fire. We
all share such moments of perfect time.

Other times, much less than perfect moments, I'm
spared. Someone else is there to take my place. I do not
see my son when he returns bloodied and incoherent.
It is the piano-man who drives the miles to town as I
sleep, unawares. The wounds are dressed, the uncon-
vincing explanations planned and when I awake there is
a song written, to be sung and then filed with other fam-
ily memorabilia of emergency rooms and drunken, bleed-
ing kids. So glad to have the song and not true memory, just
for once.

Other nights are not so easy. There's one without a moon,
when the snow is the only lightness and I'm alone when my son
comes home. His face is very white when it should be red from
cold. He staggers, not seeming to comprehend the presence of the
wall, yet the pore-soaking, sickly sweet smell of alcohol is not with
him. He stares at me, wild-eyed with confusion and fear as I stare
at him, trying to determine what has taken him to this place he's in.
I lead him to the couch, lay him down, and over-feed the fire as he
begins to shake.

"Hold me, Mum," he shouts and clings to me as his body convuls-
es. I am using my spirit. I am willing it to bind around my son like
a tight, silken-thread cocoon, to hold the shattered pieces of my
child in place; to keep him from spraying off into places of no
return. We don't hear the piano-man as he comes in from the
night and perhaps I don't see him immediately as he stands at

the entrance to the room, watching. My eyes tell him to leave and I hear him walk outside, down the wooden steps and away across the snow. There is no need to explain or to apologize to him who had no place there on that night.

————————

I didn't plan on waking up one afternoon, forty-seven years old and newly divorced for the third time. I didn't plan on having no money and no job, a big habit and heavy debts to all the wrong people in town. It's not how my life was meant to be. When I arrived in Florida I was in great shape, with a great job in one of the best piano bars in town. I used to cycle along the boardwalk every morning with my kid in a seat behind me and it felt like this was just the beginning.

My wife, the first one, worked days. I worked nights, except it wasn't like work, it was like one big party night after night after night. It's hard to keep a marriage going when your partner is working out the next day, while you're still sleeping off the day before. People go on vacation and they can do this for a week, a month and then they go home and get back in sync' but when it's your regular job, your regular life that parties on 'til three and four a.m., nights run into weeks, months, years. Faces keep changing like on the photo op. boards; stick your head through this hole and get your picture taken. You can be whatever you want. You can be a Neanderthal dragging your wife along by the hair or you can sit in a piano bar for a few hours. Either way the civilized part gets hidden away, forgotten.

Everyone loves the piano-man and sooner or later he doesn't know one face from the other but that doesn't matter because he's found a way to stay in party mode and that's what he's getting paid for. I didn't even know I was hooked. I just kept telling myself that it was all part of the job but the order had changed and I wasn't using coke to support my work anymore, I was working to support my habit.

When I skipped town, went up north, Ontario, to my grandmother's place, she couldn't handle my white skin! She doesn't catch on as quick as she used to and she kept on asking me where I'd been for the last twenty years, couldn't understand living in Florida and never seeing the sun so, I invested in some 'Kwik Tan' before heading east. By this time I'm ready to work again, maybe write some of my own material like I used to. All I need is a quiet place until I get back on track and my uncle owes me so I move in with him which is okay except his live-in is pure hill-billy and I don't need that kind of stress.

My uncle's neighbour wasn't really looking for a boarder but we hit off and she seems to enjoy the company. I'm keeping things purely platonic, no complications and it works; my landlady's my best friend. She doesn't ask questions, takes me for what I am and now that I've got a job in town, things are really picking up.

It's not a great bar I'm working, not a great neighbourhood but Friday nights are busy and the tips aren't bad. It's a start. The woman I live with has come to watch me play. She's the only unattached female in the place, until the woman in the pink dress arrives. This woman is planning on taking home a man, no mistake and she scans the herd, trying to decide which one she's going for. She only buys her first drink. Second one arrives at her table and she smiles at the guy who sent it over, just a little non-committal smile, it's too early to play favourites and she's keeping all her options open. Obviously she's done this before and she can put the word out in letters ten feet high, with just one look. Sure, she starts sending messages my way and yes, I play along because it's part of my job to make everyone feel good, but I'm not really interested. I played that game too long already, it's one of the habits I gave up when I moved out here.

I was planning on staying around, maybe even developing a relationship with the landlady except that half-way through my second set I notice she's not around anymore and by the end of the third set I'm realizing that I don't have a ride home. I've been ditched! So, I check out the woman in the pink dress. It doesn't look like she's made her final pick yet so I play a slow number that's never failed me yet. It's called, 'Tonight an angel walked into my life'.

————

The bar scene is not for me. The scarred piano, not perfectly in tune, does nothing for his music and after the first set I'm bored. The woman in the pink dress is a welcome diversion. With broad strokes she paints her message clearly and within minutes she has every man in the place casting sideways glances. They start showing off or getting 'cool' and I feel like it's prom night all over again. Some of the men are positively panting. This woman is amazing, she has them mesmerized by the chasm of raw sexuality that's covered by the close fitting, high necked, not too short, pink dress.

Eventually she follows me to the washroom. She comes not to pee but to question me.

"Your man?" she asks, then flips the question into a statement as she continues, "he sure can play piano".

I look at her carefully. She is not very pretty and her waist is thicker than the dress demands. She has a hurt and hungry look but I sense she plays by the ancient rules of sisterhood.

"He's not my man," I tell her and she smiles.

I slip away from the bar with an unexpected surge of relief. The moon is risen and full and as I drive away from the city my relief turns to joy. The State of Grace is over, this I know but its residue is with me, a reinstated memory with many recipes. At home, in the mystery of midnight, I dance on the shore with my shadow, the skim of ice crumbles under my feet and everything shines silver.

Search for the Second Crow

I've grown tired of counting crows
in this place where life has led to
of searching, always searching
for a second set of wings

I stumble over talismen
hoarded from the past
gathered to protect, prevail
detritius of dreams, all doomed to fail

I'm tired of counting crows
and I cast these objects from me
shining stones and shards of glass
feathers, icons cast in brass

For too many years I held them
kept them long enough
these days I choose to plot my course
without a constant call to unknown force

and when a single crow appears
I know Crow One is gone
(dangles on a stick above some corn
playmate of the wind and things forlorn)

It's Second Crow who now presides,
takes precedence, provides
Joy! to bleach out sorrow's stain
Joy! invited to remain.

SEARCH FOR THE SECOND CROW

Swimming with the
Philos Logos Fish

Chicken wire, she discovers is another of life's disappointments. It doesn't mold into shape as easily as she had anticipated and its structural integrity equals that of wet cardboard. She had expected strength, manageability and she had not expected to be scratched deeply, recurrently as she tried to wrestle the recoiling roll in to obedience. Only when she has scurried crab-like, while still retaining feet and a hand in strategic positions, when her free hand has reached out and grasped the tape's smooth, familiar surface and she has heard the reassuring, moist tearing sound of its readiness; only then does she dominate the chicken wire, forcing it finally to maintain the shape that she insists upon.

She cannot remember life before duct tape and doesn't want to anticipate life without it but she is well aware that Nigel doesn't share this love of hers. She notices early in their relationship that duct tape is one of the few essentials not present in his large and cherished box of tools. She tries to get him hooked, shortly after their first date, when he attempts to repair her geriatric washing machine.

This machine has been groaning longingly for its final, final rinse cycle for long enough and wants only to gyrate off to some celestial laundromat. She knows quite well how to make deals with crotchety old appliances, how to play for time: pretty please, just ten more loads, just one more month! but she is flattered by this gallant Mr. Fix-it who sincerely wants to help. Also, she is too new to the relationship, too shy to push him away when he begins to consult the tattered manual, twisting the dials, carefully listening to the mysterious clicks, gently squeezing the various hoses as if they were blocked intestines.

"A little tape might do it", she suggests, peering over the up-turned washing machine at the man trapped behind it, sitting in a pool of greasy water. "You can usually fix anything with duct tape", she falters off.

"Yes," he replies in his deep, serious voice, "or you can do it right the first time." His tone is neither supercilious nor smug but from this moment on, whenever he encounters scurrilous grey wads of tape during his various forays into decrepit appliance repair and general home maintenance, she cringes silently. This does not stop her from continuing to buy the economy, three roll bulk pack.

After she has coerced the chicken wire into the shape required she hides it in the bedroom. They are not yet lovers so it will be easy to hide it from him there.

Still in the bedroom she dresses for town, negotiating carefully around the shape which commandeers most of the available free space. The new curtains shift gently in the breeze just as she planned and she is glad of the tiny shells which touch together occasionally, producing their own certain sound.

This attention given to the curtains now leads to the previous night's dreaming. This is a regular occurrence, the convenience of forgetfulness interrupted by the insistence of memory. The dream has a shocking, numbing effect. She is glad it is the day of her appointment and she notes the coincidence, wondering if her psyche has become as some precocious child, having learnt to demand attention in irrefutable ways. Herself, she feels it is time to stop; after five years of delving and probing into painful places she is bored with introspection. She wants to be present and uncomplicated.

The doctor refers to his notes from the previous visit. He's a big man, solidly built with especially large head and hands. His sensuous mouth is partially hidden by the full beard he wears and Gilda suspects that he would look quite boyish without it. As it is she is comfortable with his gentle dignity, which she senses comes naturally from a place of true compassion. She notes the similarities in appearance between Nigel and the doctor and wonders briefly whether this might constitute part of the attraction, a need to gravitate towards something known, something trusted.

The doctor reads her previous statement, searching for a point of re-entry into the realms of her perception. He reads: *I was walking on the beach, just wallowing in the essence of sun and sand and sea. Then I*

*noticed some pebbles that seemed to be moving. I looked more closely and
saw that it was crab shells full of writhing maggots that had caught my eye.*

"You said that this reminded you of Gunther Grass, his horse's
head full of eels, and you felt that the symbolism was the same."

He continues to read: *I walked farther and saw an eroded periwinkle shell
which reminded me of my own nipple, frozen and bloodless. I thought of the
prophets and how they translated everything into signs of things to come. I decid-
ed that they were probably right, that everything in* The Bible *is probably true.*

"Do you still think this?" The doctor asks her a direct question.

"I can think of eels writhing in a head or I can think of them swim-
ming to the Sargasso Sea for mating. I'm beginning to realize that
I do have a choice," Gilda replies.

The doctor nods his head comfortably and pushes his notes to
one side while asking, "And how are you sleeping? Are you
remembering any dreams?"

Gilda begins to relate the dream she has remembered from
the night before, beginning with the curtain shifting soft-
ly, sensitive to subtle shifts in the night air. She pushes
the curtain aside and walks along the path towards the
moon which sparkles on the water. The pathway turns
to stone and a child takes her hand.

"We open a gate and enter a snow-covered garden.
There's a house with a black door and we wait for the
door to open. I look back at our footprints in the snow.
An old, speechless woman leads us inside, her head
turned off to one side in an attitude of fear or shame. She
leaves us in a sterile white kitchen where a tall, matriar-
chal woman announces disdainfully that our services will
not be required.

My young companion is devastated, she does so want to please and just as she is about to cry a man enters. He is cheerful, sympathetic and sure that he can find something for us to do. In the dream our sense of relief is only momentary before the pace quickens and disjointed images flicker by, generated by some ghastly magic lantern ... achair achild aman a chair a child a man a child a man a child a child. The images slow then cease and we are in the big kitchen again, just me and the child and we're trying to wipe it clean. The secretions are invisible but we can't wipe them away.

Then, the two women of the house come back. We know they can see the slimy stuff that's everywhere but they pretend it's not there and make us tea and feed us cookies."

The doctor has listened carefully to the dream and when it's over he raises his brows slightly as if to re-focus his eyes. Gilda anticipates his question and continues.

"Of course I know exactly what it means. I recognize the people, the two women and the man. They used to own the grocery store on the street where I lived; a man, his mother and his wife. The man was always very friendly and the women always cold and distant. Not hard now, to understand why.

When I was five or six I went through a stage of pilfering from my own money box. I'd developed a weakness for fondants, little squares of sponge covered with icing. They were sold at the grocery store but my mother never bought them, insisting that home baking was best. Fine, except she never made fondants, which of course made them even more desirable. It became quite a feeding frenzy. I was buying cakes six, ten at a time, taking a couple of bites from one, a nibble from another and so on. They were very sweet as I remember and I couldn't eat them all so I shared my left-overs with the other kids. Imagine us, a huddle of scruffy little mill-town kids pigging out on Sunday best, company's-coming cakes, day after day after day.

Of course, the grocer must have known right off that the cakes were our forbidden fruit; I mean technically the money was mine, given by aunts and uncles to be hoarded up for holiday treats, but he probably thought I was taking it from my mother's purse like other kids did. Guilt was the hook. That's how he reeled me in to his house, ostensibly to discuss how we would explain it to my parents, I'm sure. And me, so eager to prove that I was really not a naughty girl, would do as I was told. I'm only surprised that it took so long for me to remember exactly how much those cakes cost."

"Do you have any doubts?' the doctor queries.

Gilda is certain and doubts only her lack of grief, her sneaking regard for the shopkeeper's audacious manipulation. Yes, she acknowledges this is the memory that crouched in the packing cases, behind the unopened doors and along the endless corridors of her dreams. She is glad to have it in her grasp finally; not to use as some filial adornment, a badge of ravaged sisterhood but simply to discard in the gutter.

Gilda has been working on the shape. She flakes away the dried flour paste which adheres to her hands and arms like ancient skin. The shape is almost completed. It dominates all space in the bedroom. One of the fins stretches out across her bed and sometimes, on a restless night she touches it with her foot as she turns. She wants it to dry quickly but as well as the wire and the tape she has used two litres of white glue, almost seven kilograms of flour, two weeks' supply of newspaper from three separate households and all the water it takes to unite them as a whole. She wants to move the shape, hide it somewhere else so she can invite Nigel into her inner sanctum. She wants to have him in her bed but her desire is tempered by her need to keep the shape well hidden.

Artists will find ways of gaining recognition, even while feigning modesty, affecting anonymity. Gilda and Nigel met because they were meant to. It was the gentle hand of Fate that set them on a collision course and Fate, anxious to receive full credit, devised the most unlikely scenario to bring Gilda and Nigel together. There can be no doubt, it was the gentle hand of Fate that cracked the glass in Gilda's large fish tank one night as she lay sleeping.

Nigel took the call for help. He wasn't actually working that day but he loved fish so much that he usually went to the store on his days off and pottered around the fish room. It wasn't desire to sell the largest aquarium in stock that prompted him to load it in his van and hurry over to Gilda's; he simply wanted to save the fish. This he did and only because they were cichlids he explained and particularly hardy ones at that.

"They're also pugnacious and difficult to breed," he told her, "would much rather make war than love."

"So how then?" she wanted to know and so began a long meander about marine reproduction which led eventually with the eels to the Sargasso Sea.

Since that morning Gilda's life changed. Not just because there was a man in it but because of the eels.

"They all swim there," he'd explained, "every single eel in the world goes to the Sargasso Sea to meet and mate."

Perhaps Nigel wouldn't have said more. Over the years he'd become careful with his wealth of knowledge, fearful of sounding tedious but because of Gilda's obvious interest he continued.

"There are two species of eel; North American and European and all the fry begin their journey from the Sargasso. The interesting thing is that the European eels never swim to America and the American eels don't go to Europe."

"But how can they know?" questions Gilda, now completely fascinated and glowing with primal love for the billions of baby eels being whirled around the planet by the Gulf Stream.

It is at the moment when Nigel explains how the American eels mature earlier, become strong sooner and able to leave the clutch of current, to swim off towards their proper home, while the European eels, still helpless, are carried farther towards their point of destiny; it is at this very moment that the final piece falls into place, that life for Gilda becomes whole.

The full impact of this new knowledge didn't become apparent until that night. Nights for Gilda were long and often filled with dread. She'd taken to sleeping on the floor, avoiding her bed, hoping to trick insomnia, to circumvent nightmare. As she lay on the floor, body hunched into a tight foetal ball, down comforter already twisted tightly around her, thoughts of eels, billions of baby eels begin to swirl around in her head and then it was the Gulf Stream that was swirling, like an endless shimmering scarf and then all the planets were spinning together in a perfect choreography and she smiled in the darkness at the beauty of it all. Tears of pure joy flowed gently as she lay on the floor and gazed through the window at the stars.

Gilda is painting the shape. It will be painted in every beautiful colour and it will shimmer, she has decided. She mixes silvered powders with the indigo and magenta and blends metallic gold with electric yellow and Chinese red. There are many coats of paint. There is intricate detail: a zillion dots, swirls and spirals; much paint, many brushes and enough time taken to convince Nigel that he may never see the inside of her bedroom door. This is not part of the plan, this is just a wrinkle. She

125

knows they will share her bed, will drift off together to their own special sea but until then she has to restrain herself, has to pull away from him at strategic moments and ask if he would like more tea.

The final touches of paint are almost dry and she glues the tiny squares of coloured glass into place, painstakingly, one after one after one. They gleam in the light of her bedside lamp. Sprinkles of glitter powder also catch the light. Some has spilt on the quilt which, she notices, is also splattered with paint and has one errant strip of duct tape clinging grimly to it, as duct tape will. She removes the tape but the paint and the sparkles will have to stay. There's no time for laundry, tonight is finally the time. It is his night to work late, but soon he will arrive.

"I have something for you," she says almost immediately. "You'll have to come into my bedroom for it."

His heart hovers, mid leap. Yes, the words he's longed to hear but the directness of her approach dismays him. Nigel hesitates in the hall. Gilda stands by the bedroom door and looks back at him.

"Come on!" She reaches out her hand and pulls him into the room.

His way is blocked by the largest fish he's ever seen that glitters and gleams, a brilliant array of colour and decoration. He's astonished.

Gilda is drinking in his reaction like a weary desert traveller and there's a pause, almost like the cup ran dry too soon.

"It's a Philos Logos Fish," she begins, voice faltering slightly, tinged with a nuance of doubt. "I wanted to give you something as beautiful as you gave me when you told me about the eels. Philos was a philosopher in the fourth century B.C. who believed that everything in the universe is part of one big plan, a Logos."

"A Philos Logos Fish." Nigel repeats the words slowly, gradually recovering his composure and reaching out to touch the alluring surface of the papier mache. "It's more beautiful than any fish I've ever seen before."